Mark McKnight was born in Lisburn, Northern Ireland. He is an author, a teacher, a musician, a missionary and a filmmaker in that order. Hopefully, this arrangement will change in the not too distant future. He currently lives in Northallerton, North Yorkshire (England) but in his own words, "It's not Ireland and it's not Africa!" He has told and written a plethora of short and longer stories, including *Msimulizi: Stories for Mwangaza, Msimulizi 2: The Green Dragon* and *500: A Collection of Very Short Stories.* He is also co-author of *On The Road: The Official Story of the First Mwangaza Children's Choir*

The Village At The End Of The World
is his fifth printed work.

Forthcoming and already available titles
by Mark McKnight

Msimulizi: Stories For Mwangaza
Msimulizi 2: The Green Dragon
Msimulizi 3: (As Yet Untitled)

The Village At The End Of The World

500: A Collection of Very Short Stories

On The Road

Dude, Where's My Church?

For more copies of this book, for other titles (including CDs and DVDs), information and contact details, please visit

http://www.babymosquito.com

At the time of press, Mark McKnight is affiliated with Africa Renewal Ministries and the Mwangaza Children's Choir. All proceeds from this book will go towards Mark's continuing work as a missionary and humanitarian worker to the children of East Africa.

the village at the end of the world

mark mcknight

Baby Mosquito Books

Acknowledgments

My most heartfelt gratitude is for Almighty God for pulling me out of that car wreck. Thank God 'On A Stormy Tuesday Afternoon' is just a story.

Then in no particular order, thanks are also due to Adam Ansel, my several families, the village and particularly the children of Gaba, NLBC, the staff and pupils of Applegarth P.S., Baz & Vix, Craig & Vivienne, Mark & Andrea, Pete, Jeff and Pizza Figaro.
And to everyone who has been an encouragement, an inspiration or a muse for my creativity: I thank you.

Copyright © 2006 by Mark McKnight
First published in 2006 by Baby Mosquito Books

The right of Mark McKnight to be identified as the Author of the Work has been asserted by him in accordance with the Copyright, Designs and Patents Act 1988.

ISBN 1-905691-04-1
ISBN 978-1-905691-04-3

This book has been typeset in
Arial, Times New Roman, Running Smobble, Samarkan, Orbus Multiserif, Celtic, Celtic Eels, American Uncial, Dinner, Diploma, Raindrop Splash, Braggadocio, FranciscoLucas Llana, Freebooter Script, Doctor, Luna Bar, Big Log & Ashley
Fonts supplied by http://www.dafont.com
Graphics supplied by Microsoft Office Online

Printed and bound in Great Britain by Lightning Source Inc, Milton Keynes
Printed and bound in the U.S. By Lightning Source Inc, LaVerne, TN

Mark McKnight
87 Killowen Grange
Lisburn
Co. Antrim
BT28 3JE
NORTHERN IRELAND

http://www.babymosquito.com
mark@babymosquito.com

For Pete
Surely this is the end?
One is a gesture, two a generosity.
Three is extravagant, four is extraneous.
And what of five???
Rev. 2:10

And For Craig
because you never made me pay what I owe:
much more than a debt of pounds and pence!
You have taught me more than how to be a techie.
You have given me more than just malaria.
Matt. 25:35-36

May the light
always find
you on a
dreary day.

When you need to
be home, may you
find the way.

May you always
have courage to
take a chance.

And never find
frogs in your
underpants.

An Irish Blessing

mark mcknight

contents

9

the village at the end of the world

the big city

the village at the end of the world

prologue

Have you ever lived in a village, and a small city doesn't count? You city folks just won't understand. This tale is not for you city types. Maybe we'll let you read on so you can join in the fun, but this tale is really for the boys and girls from the villages. Because *we* know what it's like to grow up away from the hustle and bustle of the city. It's a simpler, more innocent way of life. If you aren't a city slicker, you'll know what I'm talking about.

Our story is about a very special village: a very special village with a very special name. The village's name was 'The Village At The End Of

The World.' Of course, you're going to tell me that there is no end of the world – long ago, science told us that the world is round but our story takes place in a time when people still believed that the world was flat so as far as anyone knew, the villagers really did live at the end of the world.

Let me explain. The city was far, far away. So far, in fact, that it would take you two whole years to travel from the big city to the Village At The End Of The World. So far, in fact, that only five people had ever made the trip to the Village At The End Of The World and each one of those five people now lived in the Village At The End Of The World. In fact, they were the only people who lived in the Village At The End Of The World. It was a VERY small village. To get there, just follow Village At The End Of The Road Highway for two years and when the road drops into the ocean, look for the 5 houses in a circle by the side of the road. That's the Village At The End Of The Road.

But as time went by, the Village At The End Of The World just seemed to grow and grow and grow...

a lion for mayor

Once upon a time, there was a lion who was caught in a very unfortunate trick. In some ways, it was his own fault – he would spend so much time chasing butterflies, someone was bound to get angry with him.

You see, there was a princess who really loved the butterflies and when she saw how much our friend the lion disturbed her friends (the butterflies) she decided to play a trick on him.

She challenged him to a competition of walking – it was a race to see who could be the first to walk to the end of the world and come back again in the shortest time. The princess sent the lion in one direction and she started off in the other direction. Unfortunately for the lion, it was a trick and once he was out of sight, the princess stopped walking and came back to play with her butterflies – she knew that since there was no end

of the world, the lion would never reach it and since he would never reach the end of the world, he would never be able to turn around to come back. The princess knew that she would never have to see the mean old lion again.

Little did the princess know that in two years time, the lion would reach the Village At The End Of The World. Luckily for both the princess and the butterflies, something very interesting happened soon after the lion arrived to make him want to stay.

Two years traveling did what it would do to any self-respecting carnivore. It made him hungry. It made him HUNGRY. It made him

HUNGRY!!!

And what does a carnivore like to eat? Meat, meat and more meat. Zebra, wildebeest or gazelle would have been fine but there was a big, big problem. For now, there was nothing for a lion to eat in the Village At The End Of The World. The only meat for a hungry lion to eat around here was human beings and he was really hungry. The lion began to look for a nice human to eat but being a slightly old lion, he decided that he didn't want to have to try to eat an adult – they would put up much too good a fight. A baby would be much easier to kill and eat.

Mr. Lion began looking into the houses in the Village At The End Of The World to try to find a nice juicy baby to eat. Now, something you must know is that people in the Village At The End Of The World were very, very, very strong. Even babies. Nobody really knew why, it just seemed to be that people who lived there never got sick. And they never died. They never hurt themselves or broke their arm or caught the flu or had a headache and they were really, really strong. Mr. Lion didn't realize this of course, and when he found this nice, juicy baby sleeping in her crib, he began to lick his lips in anticipation.

Although the baby was just three months old, she could already walk, run and even swim. The baby awoke while the lion was still licking his lips and deciding how he was going eat the child. As soon as the baby saw the lion, she jumped out of her crib, ready to fight. The first thing the baby did was to punch the lion, right on the end of his nose. The lion, not being used to his prey fighting back like this, immediately began howling. Not roaring like a king of the jungle about to catch his prey, but like a little baby crying for him mommy! In fact, the lion was like a baby and the baby was like a lion.

While the lion was crying, the baby ran outside so that there would be more room to have a proper fight. The lion soon pulled himself together and decided that he wasn't going to let his lunch get away so easily. He ran outside to find where the baby had gone. The baby had waited just outside the door for the lion to arrive and as soon as the lion came out the door, she jumped from behind a rock and stamped on the poor lion's paw. This time, the lion didn't start to cry but he did get angry. He got really, really angry – no little baby was going to get away with doing that kind of thing to a lion. After all, what would the lion's friends think?

The lion decided that enough was enough and this time he was going to get the baby. The baby began running away but a baby who was only three months old was no match for a lion and he soon caught up with her. He was about to sink his sharp teeth into the baby when suddenly, the baby stopped and began to talk.

"Hello Mr. Lion. How are you today?" said the baby.

"I'm fine but I'm feeling very hungry," said the lion.

"Is that why you keep trying to eat me?"

"Well, to begin with, yes. But you keep being so mean to me by punching me on the nose and stamping on my paw that now I would be very happy to eat you to pay you back for all the mean things you've done to me."

"Eating me doesn't seem very fair for me."

"It's not meant to be fair for you. You're a baby and I'm a lion. I'm at the top of the food chain so you better get used to the idea!"

"But this is the Village At The End Of The World. You can't just come along and eat people whenever you feel like it."

"What did you say?"

"I said, you can't just come along and eat people whenever you feel like it."

"No, no, no. You said something about the end of the world."

"Oh, you're right. I said, 'This is the Village At The End Of The World. You can't just come along and eat people whenever you feel like it.' That's what I said."

"Why is it called the Village At The End Of The World?"

"Err…because it's a village and it's at the end of the world. Umm, you're not really a very smart lion, are you?"

"Be quiet. I'm eating you. I've decided and that's that!"

"Well, that's quite up to you but you'll have to catch me first," said the baby and with that, she ran to the edge of the ocean, jumped in the water and began to swim as fast as she could. The villagers (the other four people who lived in the Village At The End Of The World), who had seen nothing of what had happened before, saw the baby jump in the water and start swimming and immediately began to panic because everyone knew that the Village At The End Of The World was at the end of the world (Duh!). In fact, the Ten Commandments in the Village At The End Of The World go like this:

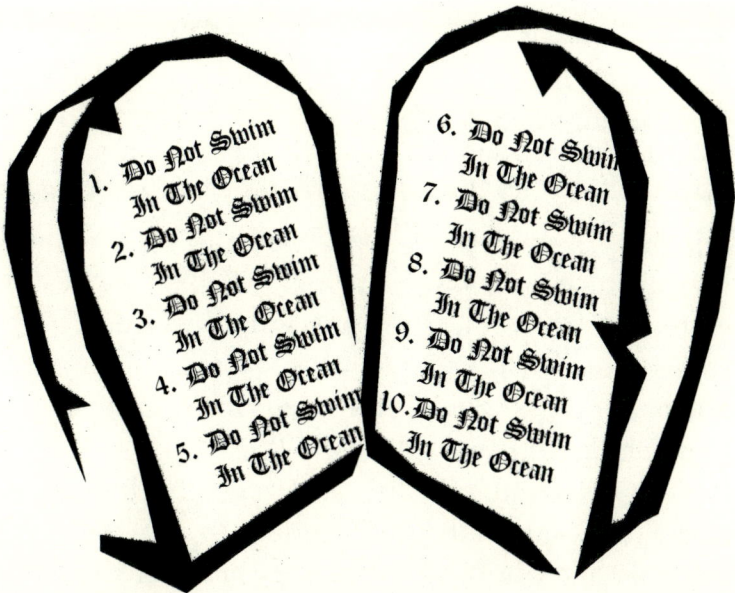

1. Do Not Swim In The Ocean
2. Do Not Swim In The Ocean
3. Do Not Swim In The Ocean
4. Do Not Swim In The Ocean
5. Do Not Swim In The Ocean
6. Do Not Swim In The Ocean
7. Do Not Swim In The Ocean
8. Do Not Swim In The Ocean
9. Do Not Swim In The Ocean
10. Do Not Swim In The Ocean

And why do we not swim in the ocean? Because if we swim in the ocean, we are likely to fall off the edge of the world and that is certain to be not much fun! It would probably ruin an otherwise happy day in the Village At The End Of The World. However, a three month old baby cannot be expected to remember the Ten Commandments. You would think, though, that she would have remembered at least one of them.

Do you think any of the other four villagers from the Village At The End Of The World jumped into the ocean to rescue the poor baby who would soon fall off the end of the world? Of course not – they had been good little boys and girls in the Village At The End Of The World

19

Sunday School and had learned their Ten Commandments off by heart.

Our friend the lion knew nothing of the Ten Commandments of the Village At The End Of The World, or even of the Village At The End Of The World Sunday School. All he knew was that this juicy, fat baby who was meant to be his lunch was swimming away from him and his chances of eating anything, never mind a baby were getting smaller and smaller by the minute. So the lion jumped into the ocean and began swimming to try to catch up with the baby.

Oddly enough, the baby and the lion soon came to a waterfall in the middle of the ocean. I have no idea how it happened, but there it was, right there – a waterfall right in the middle of the ocean. As soon as the baby saw the waterfall, he remembered the first commandment. Actually, he remembered all ten but the first was the most important for now.

"Aaaaaaaaarrrrrrrgggggghhhhh!!!!!

HHHHEEEEELLLLPPPP!!!!!!!

I'm about to fall over the end of the world. I'm a bad, bad baby who forgot the Ten Commandments. I didn't remember a single one of them and now I'm in big trouble. HELP!!!

Mr. Lion was not so badly brought up as you might imagine. In fact, he was well brought up by his lion parents and he had been taught that if someone was in trouble, he must always help them. When he heard the baby screaming for help, he immediately swam to rescue her. After all, what kind of a lion would leave a poor baby to die by falling over the end of the world? That way, he wouldn't get any dinner. The lion ever so gently took the baby in his mouth and swam back towards the shore where the villagers were very carefully watching what was going on.

By the time the lion crawled back onto the beach with the baby in his mouth, he was exhausted and lay down to rest in the sand before he began his lunch − after all, he would need to find some potatoes or something to eat with his baby. Before he could even begin thinking about his lunch, he was soon surrounded by the other four villagers.

"Wow, did you see that?" said the first. "Oh yeah, it was incredible," said the second.

"I mean, it was totally amazing," said the third.
"I have a great idea," said the fourth.
"What is it?" said the first.
"What is it?" said the second.
"What is it?" said the third.
"I think we should make this lion our mayor," said the fourth.
"What?" said the first.
"What?" said the second.
"What?" said the third.
"No, seriously," said the fourth. "Our big problem the whole time we've been here is that we don't have a mayor. Nobody to kiss babies during election season, nobody to open new shopping centres and most importantly, nobody to take care of local matters. Here we have someone who has proved his honour by saving one of our citizens. Who better to be our mayor than the king of the jungle?"

The other three villagers had to agree with the fourth – he made a very strong case. The baby, who all this time had been trying to argue that the lion wanted to eat him, was overruled since she was too young to vote. However, the three villagers first made the lion promise three things before he could become mayor. The first villager made the lion promise that no matter how hungry he was, he would never eat a human being. The second villager made the lion promise that he would always fight to protect anyone who was a proper citizen of the Village At The End Of The World. The third villager made the lion promise that he would never try to go back to the city because a village is never going to develop if it doesn't have a mayor.

And with that, the lion was proclaimed 'Honourable Mayor of The Village At The End Of The World.' No mayoral chain was needed since the lion already wore his own mane which was much more beautiful than any gold chain that a mayor could wear and that was how a lion became mayor of the Village At The End Of The World!

a hunter's last hunt

Back in the city, there lived an old, retired hunter. I'm sure you've seen pictures of these men: he always wore khaki shorts and a pith helmet. He had a very long, droopy moustache which he waxed every morning and that came to a very sharp point. I wouldn't like to get myself caught on the end of his moustache – it might hurt me! In his life, there had been several passionate romances with some beautiful women but only one of these had ended in marriage for this particular hunter. It was probably due to the fact that his best friend was a twelve guage shotgun.

Inside this hunter's house was really rather gruesome. The heads of many of the animals he had shot were mounted on the walls. All over his house were the heads of different animals hanging on the walls. In the hallway was a very handsome zebra. In the living room was a mean looking crocodile. In the kitchen was a somewhat startled looking buffalo. In the bathroom was a very stupid looking donkey (although why the hunter felt he needed to shoot a donkey, we shall never know!). At the bottom of the stairs was the beginning of a giraffe but the neck was so long, you had to climb all the way to the top of the stairs to see the giraffe's face. The hunter's pride and joy was an enormous elephant's head which hung in the bedroom. It was so big that it almost took up the entire wall. Yes, this particular hunter had been very successful. You could probably fill up an entire zoo with all the animals that this hunter had killed in his lifetime.

However, there was one animal that the hunter had never been able to kill, and that was a lion. He had been saving a place on the wall of his dining room all these years for the lion's head that he hoped he would some day own. It just seemed that there was never a lion around when you needed one and if there are no lions around, it's kind of hard to shoot one! Nowadays, the hunter was an old man. Maybe you think forty is old, or maybe you think fifty is old but this hunter was sixty years old – an old, old man. His eyes had grown dim and his hands shook too much to hold his gun. Before, nothing made him happier than when he was crawling through the jungle stalking his prey. These days, he was much more likely to be found sitting in front of the fire with a cup of tea and a nice big cream bun. He used to be famous for crossing the desert on a camel. These days he found it difficult to cross the hallway in his slippers to boil the kettle! He was now a retired hunter and his much loved shotgun hung on two hooks above the fireplace.

I'm sure you know that these days, young people think they know so much better than old people. Do you think they really do know any better? Anyway, in this strange land where lions can become mayor, children actually listened to what their parents had to say and young people didn't think they knew it all. Often young hunters would visit the old, retired hunter to get his advice, to listen to his stories, to keep him up to date on the news and to bring him the most recent copy of his favorite magazine, 'Twelve Gauge Weekly.' It didn't take long for word to reach the retired hunter about the lion who had become mayor. The opportunity of a lifetime had just been presented to this retired hunter who had waited all of his life to kill a lion. Now he knew exactly where there was a lion and it was just there waiting for him.

Slowly, very slowly, he stood up from his seat and took his shotgun off the wall from above the fireplace.

 As he held the shotgun in his hands, the fire began to rekindle in the hunter's belly, his hands stopped shaking as he began what he knew would be his last hunt. When the rest of the hunters in the land heard that this old man had come out of retirement, they laughed and laughed. After all, none of them had killed a lion either – what chance did this old man have? Of course, they had all heard of the lion who had become mayor but they didn't want to travel for two years just to discover that the rumors hadn't been true.

Wilson, the until-recently-retired hunter began to gather his information. As with all rumors, particularly hunter-rumors, there was often a great deal of exaggeration. Some told him of a lion that was ten feet high and twenty feet long. Others said it had claws that were like sharpened knives and teeth like a shark. Apparently, the lion could turn a man to stone with his eyes, breathe fire from his mouth and shoot lightning bolts from his nose. His tail had to be at least fifty feet long and instead of having hair at the end, there was a huge iron ball with spikes. If you touched the lion's mane, you would instantly die because they hairs were poisoned and it would be a long, slow agonizing death because they always are, aren't they? The lion's skin was so thick that normal bullets would be useless – the only way to kill him was to find him when he was sleeping, tie his feet together and throw him in the ocean because everyone knows that lions can't swim.

We could spend hours wondering where these strange rumors start and why they are exaggerated so much. After all, you and I both know that our lion friend was just a normal sized lion who could, indeed, swim. In fact, you will remember that he was a somewhat old lion who was looking for some food which wouldn't put up a good fight. The rumors that he once ate an entire herd of buffalo or that he sometimes pounced on people just for practice seem a little extreme.

Old hunters know not to trust the stories from the young hunters so Wilson set off for the Village At The End Of The World knowing that the lion was probably just a normal lion. Unfortunately for the old hunter, no maps existed of this strange land where lions can become mayor and where children listen to their elders. When he set off on the road, he soon came to a crossroads and there stood a local farmer.

"Excuse me, kind sir," said Wilson, "would you perchance know the way to the Village At The End Of The World?"

"Certainly oi would," said the farmer, "but ye must first help me find moi sheep."

Being something of an expert in tracking animals, Wilson soon picked up the trail of the missing flock and was able to guide the farmer to his animals who were happily grazing at the side of the road.

"If you just keep follerin' this 'ere road as it goes north, in about two years ye'll find the Village At T' End Of T' Road." And so Wilson began his two year epic journey to the end of the world. Many troubles and trials faced him along the way but at length he arrived in the Village At The End Of The World.

Unwilling to waste any more time in his quest, Wilson loaded his shotgun and asked a passing man on the road, "Excuse me, kind sir, would you perchance know where your mayor is? You see, I'm a hunter and I've never shot a lion before. I'm here to shoot him. Would you be so kind as to announce my arrival?"

At that, the man began laughing. "Well, I'd be happy to announce your arrival," said the man between guffaws, "but I'm afraid I'd be wasting your time. You see our mayor is a rhinoceros. Fancy having a lion for mayor. What sort of a village would we be if we had a lion for our mayor?"

Since Wilson already had a nice rhino head mounted in his hallway, he decided that there was no point staying here any longer and once he had eaten some dinner and had a good night's sleep, he began his two year journey back to the crossroads. Many troubles and trials faced the old hunter on his way back to the crossroads where he had met the farmer.

Four years to the day, he arrived back at the crossroads and there stood the farmer leaning on a gate. A few more grey hairs and a few more wrinkles, but the hunter recognized him straight away.

"Excuse me, kind sir," said the hunter, "I've been having a little bit of a problem. I was trying to find the Village At The End Of The World and four years ago you gave me directions to go north for two years but when I arrived, I couldn't find what I was looking for."

"Ah, roight," said the farmer. "Yes, I remember ye. Ye must be looking for t' other Village At T' End Of T' World. Oi can give you directions there but first ye must help me find moi goats."

Although his area of expertise was mostly in animals of the wilder variety, the old hunter had some limited experience in domestic animals and soon found the trail of the missing goats.

"Roight," said the farmer, "thank ye kindly. If ye just keep follerin' this 'ere road as it goes south, in about two years, ye'll find the Village At T' End Of T' Road." Once again Wilson set off on his two year epic journey to the Village At The End Of The World. This road was much more difficult, had more troubles and more trials than the road that went north but at length, the old hunter arrived at the Village At The End Of The World.

Six years since the start of this quest, Wilson could not bear to waste another minute so he loaded his shotgun and found an old woman at the side of the road.

"Old woman," said the hunter, "I'm a hunter and I'm here to shoot your mayor. You see, I've never shot a lion. Would you be so kind as to introduce me?"

Instantly, the old woman began to laugh at him. "I could introduce you to our mayor, certainly. I don't think it would be much use to you though, after all, he's an ostrich. You must be a little crazy or something? What kind of a weird village would have a lion for mayor? He might eat someone!"

"An ostrich? AN OSTRICH! Why would anyone want to shoot an ostrich? They're ugly, they smell, they're… OSTRICHES!" said the old hunter. And after a good dinner and a good night's sleep the hunter decided not to waste any more time and set off back towards the crossroads.

Another two years later, the hunter once again arrived at the same crossroads and who should be standing there but the same farmer that had so far given him the wrong directions twice.

"Excuse me, sir," said the hunter, "I'm not sure if you remember me. Eight years ago you gave me directions to the Village At The End Of The World but they were the wrong directions. I came back four years ago and you once again gave me the wrong directions. I am looking for the Village At The End Of The World. The one where they have a lion for their mayor."

"Aaaaaaaaaaahhhh!!! Yes, oi remember ye all right," said the farmer, "but why didn't ye say so. Of course, ye know that there's four Villages At T' End Of T' World. There be one in the north, one in the south, one in the west and one in the east. If ye'd jest told me which one ye were looking for, oi could have sent you to the roight one. Now before oi tell ye where to go, ye must first help me find moi pigs."

Although Wilson had a little experience in the ways of sheep and goats, he had no idea of how to track a herd of pigs. Many days were wasted helping the farmer, trying to find his missing pigs. Eventually, quite by chance, Wilson spotted the pigs rolling in some nice dirt behind a hedge. With all the time wasted on the pigs, the farmer sort of forgot where he was and when he meant to tell Wilson to go east, what he actually said was, "Roight then, if you just foller this 'ere road … err … west for two years then ye'll find the Village At The End Of The World."

Thinking himself to have finally have found the way to the Village At The End Of The World, the one with a lion for mayor, Wilson once again set off on his two year journey to the Village At The End Of The World. This journey was even more difficult with more troubles and trials than the last but at length, he arrived at the Village At The End Of The World. After ten years of trying, the hunter didn't want to waste another moment so he loaded his shotgun and stopped a child at the side of the road.

"Young urchin," said the hunter, "Would you by any chance know where I could find the mayor of your village? You see, I'm a hunter and I've never shot a lion so I'm here to hunt your mayor."

The child looked very thoughtful for a while, as if he didn't understand completely. But eventually he said, "I can go and find our mayor if you want but I don't think you'll be very pleased. You see, he's a frog. A very big frog, but very definitely a frog. I don't think he even knows any lions. Wouldn't it be a little bit silly to have a lion for your mayor? I mean, what if he ate someone?"

"A FROG?!?!?!?!?" screamed the hunter. "It's been ten years since I started on this quest and so far I've had the opportunity to shoot a rhinoceros, an ostrich and now a frog. All my life I've waited for a lion and now you're telling me you're mayor is a frog..." But by that time, the child had lost interest and had run off down the street kicking a rock.

By now, Wilson was positively hopping mad. For ten years he had been trying to find this stupid lion and so far his time had been wasted by a stupid farmer who couldn't even manage to stop losing his own animals. After a good dinner and a good night's sleep, the hunter once again set off on his two year journey back towards the crossroads. When he arrived at the crossroads, the farmer, as always, was leaning on the gate.

"YOU! YOU GAVE ME THE WRONG DIRECTIONS NOT JUST ONCE, NOT JUST TWICE BUT THREE TIMES. I MEAN, ONCE IS AN ACCIDENT, TWO IS CARELESS BUT THREE TIMES? I'M BEGINNING TO THINK YOU'RE DOING IT ON PURPOSE..." the hunter shouted.

"Well sir, if ye'll be so kind a to help me find moi cows, oi can tell ye exactly where the Village At T' End Of T' World really is. Oi made a bit of a mistake the last time and oi'm very sorry for that but moi cows are missing and oi'd appreciate the help," said the farmer.

This time, Wilson was not interested in helping this simpleton to find his cows. After all, there was only one road from the crossroads left to follow. It had to be the road that led to the Village At The End Of The World. The one where they had a lion for mayor. He ignored the farmer and set off along the last road from the crossroads –

the one which led east. For two years he traveled along the road but strangely enough it was an easy journey. There were none of the trials and troubles along this road that Wilson had met while traveling north, south or west. In fact, it was the shortest two years of the entire twelve year epic.

At the end of the two years of travelling, Wilson decided to have a rest before he began to hunt the lion. He thought, 'I'll have some food and sleep a while before I begin my hunt.' He opened his knapsack and started to eat his little picnic. When he had finished, he lay down at the side of the road to have a nap in the hot afternoon sun.

While he was still sleeping, who should come along but his quarry – the lion who he had hunted for so long. For fourteen years, he had searched for this lion and now, while he was sleeping, his prey stood gazing down upon his sleeping form. What Wilson didn't realize was that the Village At The End Of The World got very cold at night and when the lion saw this old man sleeping by the side of the road, he lay down next to him, covering him with his mane so that he wouldn't freeze sleeping out in the cold.

When the hunter awoke the next morning and realized he had been saved from the midnight cold by the very lion who he wanted to mount on the wall in his dining room, he was indeed placed in a quandary. However, a hunter's instincts never really die and he grabbed his shotgun to kill the lion.

The lion was smarter than the hunter thought. Word had reached him that this hunter had been searching for him for the last fourteen years. When the lion saw the shotgun while the hunter was sleeping, he instantly knew exactly who this old man was. The lion had unloaded the shotgun and lay down to sleep, using his mane to keep the hunter warm for the night.

When the hunter aimed his shotgun at the lion and fired, nothing happened.

"Now Mr. Hunter," said the lion, "we find ourselves in an interesting position. You came here to shoot me and I saved your life yet you were still going to shoot me … Hmm, what shall we do. I obviously can't let you go back to the city – you might just come back and try to shoot me again." The lion thought about what he was going to do for just a little longer.

Eventually, the lion made his decision. The hunter was to stay in the Village At The End Of The World as the deputy mayor. His most important job was to clean the lion's teeth every morning and every evening. He would also occasionally help the lion

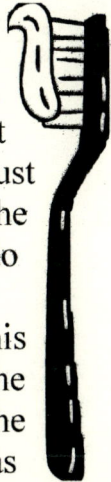

to make important decisions about village business.

And that is how the population of the Village At The End Of The World grew to an all time high of seven people: the four grown ups and baby who were there to begin with, the lion who was the mayor and Wilson, the retired hunter who was now the deputy mayor.

I'm also pleased to inform you that Wilson finally hung up his shotgun for good, although he did sometimes take the odd pot shot at a rabbit from his porch, just for old times sake.

mark mcknight

the plague of ants

Wouldn't it be nice if just for once, life was simple? Like if you got a new job that was really easy, you didn't have to do much work and could just sit with your feet up all day. Or you moved to a new place and people liked you straight away and you didn't have to try to make friends. Or when you went home after work, there was a nice warm fire to sit in front of, eat your dinner and have a nap. Or when you went to bed it didn't have any creepy-crawlies in it.

Mr. Lion (the mayor) just wanted the same things that you and I want – a simple life with an easy job, some good friends and a nice place to live. And especially, he wanted a bed WITHOUT creepy-crawlies because if there was one thing that really made Mr. Lion mad, it was creepy-crawlies. Flies, spiders, cockroaches, locusts, grasshoppers and ants were what the lion had nightmares about.

One day in the Village At The End Of The World, Mr. Lion sat behind his desk in the Village At The End Of The World village hall. Wilson, the retired hunter who was his deputy mayor, had just finished brushing the lion's teeth and they had both just settled down for their customary afternoon nap. The Village At The End Of The World only had seven residents (five if you don't count the mayor and his deputy who are at present sleeping) so there wasn't a whole lot of work for these village officials to do and so, every afternoon, they would take a well earned nap.

There's an old saying that an apple a day keeps the doctor away. Wilson, the retired hunter/deputy mayor knew this saying well and so each day he would eat an apple and throw the core out the window before he took his nap. Before long, a little pile of apple cores had accumulated outside the window. This tiny mountain of litter, which seemed so innocent to begin with soon turned into a plague of biblical proportions.

When the first two ants arrived to start eating their way through the pile of apple cores, neither the mayor nor the deputy mayor were particularly concerned. In fact, neither of them even noticed the arrival of the ants which is a shame since either one of the lion or the retired hunter could have prevented what was about to happen between snores. Nonetheless, the arrival of the first two ants went unseen and undisturbed by both of these village officials.

On the second day, the two ants were joined by two more friends – word had begun to spread amongst the ant community about the apple cores. Now there were four ants happily munching on the apple cores. Since the two new ants arrived just after lunch, once again the mayor and his deputy didn't notice the ant population increasing by one hundred percent. In fact, they didn't know that the Village At The End Of The World even had an ant population which is a shame, because this would have been a good opportunity to stop the events which are about to unfold.

On the third day, after the deputy mayor had thrown his apple core out the window and fallen asleep, another four ants arrived having heard rumors of an easy lunch but as before, the lion and the retired hunter didn't even stir from their sleep and knew nothing of the imminent disaster which was about to befall them. The ant population had now reached eight – not a plague by any standards and still a disaster that could be stopped by a single poorly placed footstep.

There is a very complicated thing called exponential increase – it means that something doubles every day. On the fourth day, eight more ants arrived making the total population sixteen. On the fifth day sixteen more arrived making thirty two. And every day the total doubled. On the sixth day there were sixty four. On the seventh day there were one hundred and twenty eight. After two weeks there were sixteen thousand, three hundred and eighty four ants. After three weeks, there were two million, ninety seven thousand, one hundred and fifty two ants all fighting over one small pile of apple cores.

At the end of just four weeks, there were two hundred and sixty eight million, four hundred and thirty five thousand, four hundred and fifty six ants and finally, the pile of apples ran out – there were too many ants and just not enough apple cores to go around. Essentially, the ants were eating them faster than Wilson could produce them. The problem with gossip is that it's easy to start but much harder to stop. As word spread about the apple cores that used to be under the deputy mayor's window but that had now run out, more and more ants kept arriving. By now, both the mayor and the deputy mayor had begun to notice what was going on and they weren't very happy. Anything that disturbed them from their afternoon nap meant they weren't very happy.

It was the middle of the afternoon of the Thursday of the fourth week since the arrival of the first two ants (which meant there were now

four billion, two hundred and ninety four million, nine hundred and sixty seven thousand,
 two hundred and ninety six ants looking for food in the Village At The End Of The World). A knock came at the door of the village hall, rudely waking both the mayor and the deputy mayor from their slumbers. It is a brave man that wakes a lion and a hunter with an itchy trigger finger. Old habits die hard: the hunter grabbed his shotgun off the wall and prepared to fire. The lion hid under the table and prepared to pounce.

In walked the old lady who you will remember as villager number four whose idea it was to make the lion their mayor. Right now, she was beginning to regret her idea all those years ago. Although, this plague of ants had been continuing for several weeks already, the mayor and his deputy had done precisely nothing and the problem with the ants was that they just kept coming.

When the ants had finished eating the apple cores, they had set out through the rest of the village in search of more food and where better to find food than in the houses of the other villagers? With so many ants, there were ants absolutely everywhere. When you got up in the morning you had to get rid of the ants before you put on your shoes. When you went to pour the milk onto your cereal in the morning, it was a risk whether you would get milk or ants. Cooking was really a waste of time. You would put some rice in a pot to cook, make sure there were no ants, put the lid on and leave it to simmer. By the time you came back, there would be no more rice – just ants. Ants in the beds, ants under the beds, ants in the kitchen, ants in the bathroom, ants everywhere. This was officially a plague. A plague of biblical proportions. No matter who was reckoning.

Of course, when the hunter saw the little old lady, he put his gun back up on the wall. After all, what sort of a hunter would shoot a defenseless little old lady? When the lion saw the little old lady, he came out from his hiding place where he was waiting to pounce. After all, what kind of a lion would pounce on a defenseless little old lady?

"Mister Mayor," said the old lady, "as our elected representative for local government, I would like to know what you plan to do about these ants that are plaguing our village. After all, you have been entrusted with civic matters in our community."

She was a very posh old lady and when she said 'ants,' it sounded like 'aunts.' That made the lion and Wilson giggle which just made the old lady even angrier.

Eventually, the little old lady managed to convince the lion and the hunter that since they were mayor and deputy mayor respectively of the

Village At The End Of The World, they really ought to do something about these ants. Yes, something had to be done. The lion and Wilson sat down to think about what they were going to do.

"We could just buy lots and lots of bug spray," suggested the lion.

"Yes but what if it killed some good bugs as well as the bad ones, like ladybirds," said the hunter.

And so they thought some more.

"We could just stamp on them," mused the hunter, "I mean, that's what we normally do with bugs…"

"Yes, we could but there's so many. We'd be so tired and our feet would hurt by the end of it," said the lion.

And so they thought some more.

All afternoon they thought and thought to try and find a solution to their problem. As it was beginning to get dark, and the lion and the hunter were really beginning to scrape the barrel with their ideas, the lion thought out loud,

"Umm … what if … err … we could … what would happen if … how about if we … uhh … just tried to talk to the ants?"

"Talk to them?" asked the hunter. This was a completely new idea to him and it might just work.

It was getting late in the day and they had missed most of their afternoon nap, so the mayor and the deputy mayor decided to wait until the next day to deal with the problem. Of course, by that time, the number of ants had doubled again – there were now eight billion, five hundred and eighty nine million, nine hundred and thirty four thousand, five hundred and ninety two ants who were now running all over the Village At The End Of The World, eating everything in sight.

When you went to bed at night, you would wake up looking at the stars – the ants had eaten the roof. In the morning, you would open your sock drawer and there would be no socks left – the ants had eaten them all. You would go to work in the morning and when you came back home, you wouldn't have a house any more – the ants had eaten it.

That's exactly what happened to the lion and the hunter. They went to bed early having missed their nap that day but when they woke up the next morning, the ants had eaten the roof of their house. And it was raining. They opened their sock drawer to get dressed in the morning but there were no socks to wear. Or any other clothes for that matter. The lion and Wilson had to go to work in their pajamas. When they arrived at the village hall to start work for the day, there was no village hall, the ants had eaten it!

The lion stood where the village hall had been and roared, "I've had enough of you ants. Where is the ant king? We need to talk." All the

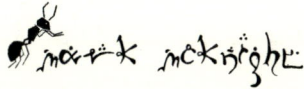

ants sent the lion to one little ant who they said was their king.

"You're the king of the ants?" said the lion.
"Well, yes," said the ant.
"You and your ants are going to eat our village out of existence."
"Well, that's not my fault," said the king of the ants.
"But you can't just eat our village," said the lion.
"Why not?" said the ant.
"Because then we'll have nowhere to live," said the lion.
"Oh. Well, we ants don't have anywhere to live. It's not really as bad as it seems," said the ant.
"Hmm…" said the lion.
"Hmm?" asked the ant.
"Hmm!" said the lion.

All of the humming was for a very good reason. You see, the lion had just had an idea which might just put an end to the plague of ants. The idea was this: the Village At The End Of The World would allow the ants to stay as long as they wanted if they promised to only eat their own food that they would grow in a field outside the village. Since there were so few people in the Village At The End Of The World and so much unused land everywhere, the lion was able to give the king of the ants an enormous field where they could live and grow their food. And since there

47

were so many ants, they were able to grow so much food that they even had some extra that they could sell to the rest of the people in the village. And do you know what they grew? They had one of the biggest apple orchards in the world – they liked the taste of the apple cores that the hunter used to throw out the window so much, that was what they decided to grow.

The ants were finally able to live in peace with the people of the Village At The End Of The World. They even made the king of the ants an honorary member of the   Village At The End Of The World Village Council and that was the the first piece of official village business that the lion who was mayor and the retired hunter who was deputy mayor had to do.

the village at the end of the world symphony orchestra

Life continued in the Village At The End Of The World: there were the five original residents including a baby, there was a lion who was mayor and Wilson, the retired hunter who was now deputy mayor and who brushed the mayor's teeth every day. There were also a whole lot of ants making their home in a field just outside the Village At The End Of The World. The ant hills were enormous! Life also continued in the big city which, you will remember, was two whole years' journey away from the Village At The End Of The World.

There was a very normal man living in the big city who went by the name of Bob. Bob had a very normal life – he wore normal clothes, ate normal food and had a normal job. I think he was probably an accountant or something. There was one thing that set Bob apart from everyone else and that was he was very lucky on his birthday. When he was five years old, he entered a competition to design a Christmas card. It was a little card with a cat looking out its window at a snowman made from cotton wool. This simple card won a prize of five pieces of silver and a didgeridoo. On his tenth birthday, Bob entered a competition to build a tower out of old newspapers. His tower was incredible – so high that he had to be the winner. For this wonderful feat, Bob won the prize of ten pieces of silver and a donkey saddle. On his fifteenth birthday, Bob entered a knobbly knees competition. And Bob's knees were so knobbly, that he was guaranteed to win. For that competition, Bob won fifteen pieces of silver and a lifetime supply of pepper and that is a prize not to be sneezed at!

On his twentieth birthday, Bob fully expected to win twenty pieces of silver and something weird, following the pattern of his other birthdays but for some odd reason, something went very, very wrong. You see, Bob was wandering along a street on his

birthday when he was stopped by a man selling tickets for a special lottery. Remembering that it was his birthday, he decided to buy a ticket – twenty pieces of silver would be very helpful, though he was worried about what the weird thing might be. Bob bought a ticket and gave the man his address so that if he won (which he knew he would) then the man could find him. Later that day, Bob was having a nap in his house when there came a knock at the door. 'That will be my prize,' thought Bob. 'I can't wait to go shopping!' Bob went to answer the door...

As soon as Bob opened his front door, the loudest music he had ever heard began to play. The man who had sold him the ticket stood there, but he had to shout to make himself heard over the sound of the music.

"BOB, I HAVE GOOD NEWS FOR YOU. YOU'VE WON OUR COMPETITION. LET ME BE THE FIRST TO CONGRATULATE YOU."

One thing Bob really loved to do was to watch movies. He especially loved to listen to the music in the movies and he always felt that the reason his own life was so normal was because there was no background music. He often wondered what it would be like if he had some kind of music to provide a soundtrack for his life. The competition that Bob had entered was a very special competition. You see, the winner of the competition would win whatever he (or she) was thinking about whenever he (or she) bought the ticket. Bob had been daydreaming about having a soundtrack for his life when he had bought the ticket off this man who was now shouting at him. The reason the man had to shout to make himself heard was because he was surrounded by a full symphony orchestra – thirty two violins, twelve violas, twelve cellos, four double basses, four flutes, four oboes, four clarinets, four bassoons, four trumpets, four trombones, four French horns, a tuba and a seven piece percussion section. Oh, and a conductor. At that moment, they were all over Bob's garden playing a fanfare to congratulate him on winning the competition.

"CONGRATULATIONS, BOB," he said, "ON WINNING OUR VERY SPECIAL COMPETITION. YOU HAVE WON YOUR VERY OWN SYMPHONY ORCHESTRA..." At that point, the orchestra began to die down a bit – they weren't playing quite so loud.

"...to perform a soundtrack for your life. Few people will have the opportunity for their life to be accompanied by any music at all, let alone a full symphony orchestra..." Unfortunately, the orchestra had been performing what we might call the calm before the storm and now chose this opportunity to reach a climax, louder than the previous one. "WELL DONE," screamed the man, "I HOPE YOU ARE VERY HAPPY WITH YOUR PRIZE." With that, the man said goodbye and left, leaving the orchestra to finish their fanfare with a flourish of trumpets and violins.

"Well, I guess you better come in for a cup of tea," said Bob as he went to his kitchen to boil the kettle. That one really stumped the conductor – the orchestra didn't know any music to accompany a kettle boiling, so he eventually agreed that the orchestra could take ten minutes break to have a cup of tea.

'What an opportunity,' thought Bob. 'I'll be the only person around with a whole orchestra to accompany my life. It will be as if I'm in the movies or something. When I fall in love, there will be beautiful music to accompany it. When something bad is about to happen to me, I'll know in advance because of the music. Wow!'

If only Bob had thought the whole thing through straight away. If only he had realized what it would mean to have an orchestra following him around. If only he had known how much tea they would drink. If only he

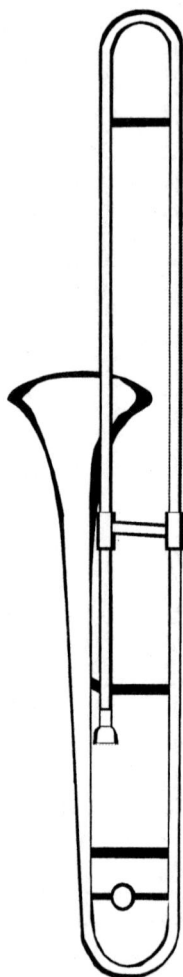

had gotten rid of them before things got so silly. But Bob was a very normal person like you or me – he didn't know what was going to happen until it was too late. He should have seen the signs. He should have listened to the warnings. He should have paid attention to his neighbor's advice on that first fateful night.

As Bob sat watching television in the evening, he was joined by the conductor, a couple of violinists and the man who played the big drum. The rest of the orchestra was relaxing in the garden since it was such a nice night. The five soon became friends, a friendship that would last for a long, long time through many troubles and trials. After some time, Bob started to get tired and decided it was time for bed. The conductor immediately lifted his baton (which is just a posh name for that little white stick that he uses to conduct) and the orchestra was assembled in next to no time. They began to play the most beautiful of lullabies – the sort that reminds you of kneeling beside your bed to say your prayers, your mummy tucking you in, your daddy kissing you on the forehead and then you hug your teddy bear until you fall asleep. It was so beautiful that even the man who played the big drum (with his hairy arms and his big red face) began to cry. Even Bob had a little sniffle before he fell asleep.

Bob had almost fallen asleep when suddenly the orchestra's music changed. It seemed to tell of an approaching doom. As if someone or something was about to knock on the front door. After just a few seconds, Bob knew that something was very, very wrong. And then he heard it…

"DING, DONG." The unmistakable chime of the doorbell. Should he answer the door? Who knows what might be out there? It might be some kind of monster – it was hard to tell from the music. Suddenly, Bob realized he was being silly – he was just a normal person. The music and the orchestra were making him feel like he was in a movie where monsters come to the door all the time. And he was not in a movie where monsters come to the door all the time. He was a normal person who wore normal clothes, ate normal food and had a normal job.

Bob put on a pair of trousers and a shirt, ignored the orchestra, and went to answer his front door. Unfortunately, since it was dark, Bob

tripped on a violin that someone had left at the top of the stairs and landed clumsily at the bottom. Shaken, but not hurt, Bob opened the front door to be confronted by his neighbor.

"Bob, you have always been a very good neighbor to me before and I have never had cause to complain but the noise from your house this evening has been too much. Now, I like a good bit of music myself but could you please just turn the volume of your..." said the neighbor. He trailed off as he saw the percussion section in the hallway.

Oddly enough, the neighbor had been out when the orchestra had first arrived so he had missed the fanfare. His complaint was about the music since Bob had gone to bed. You will remember that this particular piece had started as a lullaby and then warned of the angry neighbor coming up the garden path – nothing that really required a seven piece percussion section. However, now that the neighbor was there on the front doorstep yelling at Bob, the seven piece percussion section could really start to get going, including the man with the hairy arms and the big red face who played the big drum.

"BOB, I WANT YOU TO KNOW THAT I AM VERY ANGRY. I WILL NOT ACCEPT THIS NOISE THAT YOU ARE MAKING. IF YOU DON'T GET YOUR FRIENDS TO QUIET

DOWN, I'M CALLING THE POLICE," screamed the man, trying to make himself heard above the percussion section – drums, cymbals, the whole lot! With that, he turned around and stomped back down the garden path.

Luckily for Bob, the conductor couldn't think of anything else to play so the orchestra finished that particular piece of background music for Bob's life. By the time the conductor knew what was happening, Bob had sneaked back to bed so the orchestra decided to call it a night too.

Early the next morning, Bob's alarm rang to wake him from his slumbers. He opened his eyes and saw that his bedroom was filled with as much of the orchestra as would fit, with the conductor standing on the end of his bed. They started a very bright, happy piece to accompany him as he got ready for work. He was, after all, in a very happy mood. He had to throw the brass section out of his bathroom so that he could have a shower but they played outside the door as he washed under his arms and behind his ears. The flute players were all sitting around his kitchen table so he had to make them move before he could have his breakfast. By the time he was ready to leave, he was starting to get a little bit annoyed with the orchestra – they always seemed to be in his way

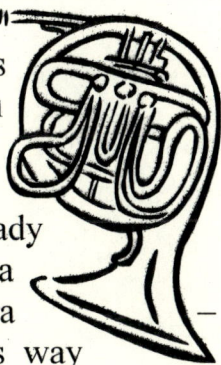

today. Since he had to leave for work soon, they wouldn't be able to follow him because they were <u>not</u> getting into his car. At lease he would get a bit of a break from them at work. So he said goodbye to the conductor, the two violinists and the man who played the big drum (with the hairy arms and the big red face) who had befriended him last night and set off for work.

What he didn't see was that just after he turned the corner out of his street, the orchestra's bus arrived to take the thirty two violins, twelve violas, twelve cellos, four double basses, four flutes, four oboes, four clarinets, four bassoons, four trumpets, four trombones, four French horns, the tuba and the seven piece percussion section to Bob's office. The conductor drove himself in a brand new sports car.

Bob had forgotten his annoyance when he arrived at his office. In fact, he had forgotten about his orchestra and was beginning to think about all the work he had to do today. Unfortunately, Bob had stopped to by a newspaper and a chocolate bar on his way to work so by the time he arrived at his office, the orchestra were already waiting for him. As he walked through the door, the conductor said, "Ladies and gentlemen, please welcome to the office, Bob." He raised his baton and began to conduct another fanfare – even louder than the one that the orchestra had played last night when Bob found out he had won the competition.

Of course, it wasn't long before Bob's boss came out of his office to see what all the noise was about. The orchestra saw him coming and changed their music – they could see that the boss wasn't happy so they started playing their angry music. That just made the boss even more angry. "Bob, is this your orchestra?" said the boss. "Well...err...yes...sort of," replied Bob. "Well then, you better keep them quiet. I can't have this kind of noise in my office. I had to fire the last person who brought an orchestra to work with them. Orchestras should be kept at home. That is company policy," said the boss.

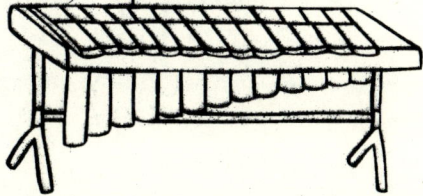

Bob was intrigued. Company policy? You mean he wasn't the first person to have his own orchestra? Had someone actually brought an orchestra into this very office before? Who were they? What was their name? How did they end up stuck with an orchestra like he now was? Where were they now? What happened to them? Why hadn't he heard about them before? A million questions raced inside Bob's head. He started to ask his boss some questions about this person who had brought an orchestra to his office, many years before.

At first, his boss seemed very reluctant to talk about the matter but Bob kept asking him more questions and he eventually gave in.

"It was about two years ago," said the boss, "just before you started working here. There was a girl who worked here who won a very strange competition. I don't know the exact details, but apparently she won an orchestra to provide a soundtrack for her life. I don't know why – her life seemed pretty normal to me."

As soon as Bob heard this, he had to know more – he knew that whatever happened, he must meet this person. Destiny was ordering that Bob should meet this girl.

"At that time," continued Bob's boss, "our company had no set policy on bringing an orchestra to the office. Nobody had ever done it before. Anyway, one day this girl (I think her name was Joy) arrived in work with a full symphony orchestra. To begin with, it was kind of novel to have an orchestra around the office. I mean, they took up a whole lot of space but it was nice to have a bit of music while we worked. Sometimes they were so loud, that we got no work done and there was never any tea left in the pot – the orchestra always drank it. Eventually, the company

changed their policy – no orchestras in the office. Orchestras should be left at home."

All this time, the orchestra had been playing light, dreamy music – the type of music you hear in a movie when someone is remembering a happy time but as soon as Bob asked his next question, the music suddenly became much more mysterious.

"But what happened to her? Where is she now?" asked Bob.

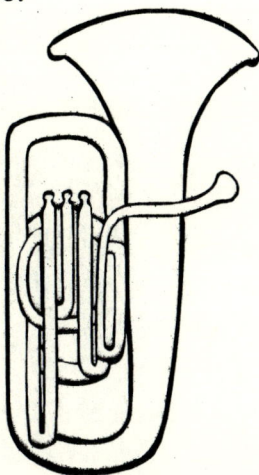

"Well, it's the strangest thing," said Bob's boss. "One day, she just disappeared. She just upped and ran off. It was the day I had to fire her – I was her boss and my boss told me that she had broken company policy too many times. I had to fire her. She just mumbled something about going to find her father and that he would know what to do. Apparently, he was deputy mayor in some village. That's all I remember really."

"But you have to tell me the name of the village. I need to meet this person," said Bob. The string section began a slow swell as the boss was trying to remember the name of the village. The brass section was getting louder and louder and louder by the minute. The seven piece percussion section was getting noisier and noisier by the minute. The man who played the big drum (with the hairy arms and the big red face) was getting redder and redder by the minute. Finally, after much thought and guesswork, the boss remembered the name of the village. At that moment, the entire orchestra reached the climax they had been waiting for so long. The strings swoll (or should that be swelled), the brass blared and the percussion crashed. It was so loud that Bob almost didn't hear the name of the village…

"The Village At The End Of The World," said Bob's boss.

'CRASH' went the cymbals. 'PAM PAM PAM PAM' went the brass section. 'DAAAAAAAAH DAH DAH DAAAAAAAH' went the string section.

Since Bob was unable to do anything about the orchestra playing non-stop in his office, his boss had no choice but to fire him. It didn't take long for Bob to decide what he needed to do. Now that he no longer had a job, he needed no prompting. In the space of an hour after being fired, Bob had packed his bags, ready for his journey – he knew he had to go to the Village At The End Of The World to find Joy and her orchestra.

The rest is just history – Bob spent the next two years on his journey to the Village At The End Of The World. When he eventually arrived, he was getting pretty fed up listening to the

'walking' music as performed by his very own symphony orchestra. Two years of the same piece of music is a bit much"

Arriving in the Village At The End Of The World, he met and fell in love with Joy who had her own orchestra providing the soundtrack for her life. Of course, when Joy and Bob met for the first time, the two orchestras joined in the most beautiful, romantic piece of music you can ever imagine.

And with that, the Village At The End Of The World's population exploded: the five original residents (including the baby that was rescued from the ocean by the lion), the lion who was mayor, the retired hunter who was deputy mayor, a whole lot of ants living in a field just outside the village, Bob, Joy and two entire symphony orchestras including two conductors and one man from each orchestra who played the big drum, each with huge, hairy arms and a big, red face.

a troop of monkeys

Monkeys are the rudest and most mischievous of animals. Some used to live in the trees around my house. They would climb in the kitchen window and eat my sausages and then they would throw coconuts at me. One monkey had even learned to say a single sentence and he would shout it at the top of his lungs to anyone who came through my gate.

"HEY, YOU SMELL LIKE A WARTHOG!" he would yell to my visitors. I didn't really mind when it was the landlord, come to collect the rent but when I was having a dinner party, it was awfully embarrassing to explain that it was my rude monkey and not me who had shouted this insult.

Contrary to popular belief, not all monkeys are rude and mischievous. Maybe all of the rude monkeys in the world just happened to be in my garden. Anyway, a group of dogs is called a pack and a group of cows is called a herd. In the same way, a group of monkeys is called a troop. This is the story of some very well mannered monkeys who were quite literally a 'troop' of monkeys.

Many monkeys are happy enough to live their lives in the trees, eating bananas and delousing one another. They wake in the morning in the cold, damp, rainforest, spend half the day looking for food and the other half trying not to get eaten by those animals privileged enough to be further up the food chain than they are. One troop of monkeys, however, decided they had had just about enough of this existence – it was time for their species to evolve, whether they liked it or not.

The old silverback in the group was in charge – he was the one who made all the decisions. Everyone called him Grandpa. After all, he was everybody's grandpa! He wasn't the sort of monkey who made these decisions lightly but recently, he had read some articles in 'Monkeys Weekly,' a magazine from the big city

about some animals that had gone to the city and
hit the big time. He had even heard about a lion
that had left the jungle and eventually become a
mayor. At great length, he decided that the troop
of monkey was going to the big city to find their
fortune. Unless you wanted a serious fight, you
didn't disagree with Grandpa and so the monkeys
did what they were told and followed the old
silverback to the big city.

Grandpa wanted to
prepare his troop of monkeys
for big city life as
thoroughly as possible so he
employed the services of a
wise old man who often
collected nuts and berries in
the forest. The old man
taught the monkeys all kinds
of strange, new things like
how to eat with a knife and
fork, how to raise your hat to passers-by on the
street and how to order from a wine list. By the
time the monkeys were ready for their move to the
big city, they were the politest, most well-bred
troop of monkeys you have ever seen – not at all
like the monkeys that used to live in my garden.
No, sir, these monkeys would never have said
something as crass as, 'You smell like a warthog.'
In fact, they would have been too polite to even
mention it if you really did smell like a warthog.

There came a day when Grandpa decided that the monkeys were ready for their move to the big city but things did not go quite as smoothly as Grandpa had hoped. You see, no matter how much you teach a monkey about good manners, he is still (on the inside) a monkey and monkeys have a very bad habit of forgetting everything you teach them. Elephants are much better animals to teach – after all, an elephant never forgets.

The monkeys arrived in the big city one bright autumn morning. The leaves were a thousand shades of yellow, red and orange and the monkeys were simply bristling with good manners. They were falling over themselves to hold doors open for people. They constantly argued about who would pay for dinner.

One of the monkeys was called Fred. He had been bored by most of the old man's teaching – he was more interested in finding mangoes to eat. He had completely missed the lesson on what to do if you see a pretty girl monkey walking down the street and right there in the middle of the big city was a pretty girl monkey, walking down the street. Fred was a very uncouth monkey and when he saw this pretty girl monkey, he knew just what to do. He immediately ran up to her and planted a big kiss, right on her cheek. For that, he was rewarded with a slap right on his own cheek from the pretty girl monkey and it wasn't long before the B.C.P.D. (Big City Police Department) arrived to arrest Fred. No matter how much Grandpa and the other monkeys protested, the police officers insisted on taking Fred to jail.

Well, that was a setback to say the least. A troop of monkeys does <u>everything</u> together. When one went to jail, that was a big, big problem but life continued as usual – the monkeys all went back to holding open doors and arguing about who would pay for dinner.

Another monkey who had been more interested in finding food than going to classes was called Big Rab. Big Rab liked his food more than anything else in the world. In the jungle, if you were hungry, you just found some bananas and tucked in. Not so in the big city, but Big Rab had missed the class on money and commerce. One day as he walked down the street, holding doors open for anyone who needed it, Big Rab started to get very, very hungry. As he passed a fruit stall in the market, Big Rab picked up a nice, ripe bunch of bananas and kept going – eating as he walked. It wasn't long before the B.C.P.D. arrived to arrest him and

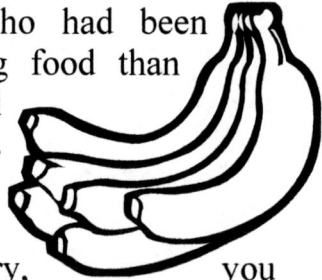

he was taken away to jail to join Fred who had still not been released.

The third monkey to fall into difficulties was called Lonely Jake. Lonely Jake was a very lonely monkey, hence his name. He just didn't seem to fit in with the rest of the group. He still did what Grandpa, the old silverback said however, so he had come to the city with the rest of the troop of monkeys.

Monkeys do a very good job of removing one another's lice but Lonely Jake didn't have many friends. Usually he did his best to remove them himself or else he scratched himself up against a tree but when he came to the big city, Lonely Jake discovered that there weren't very many trees. He decided to scratch himself up against the next best thing – a big old lamp post at the corner of the street. Unfortunately, the man who lived in the house opposite didn't like the look of what Lonely Jake was doing so he immediately called the B.C.P.D. who were soon on the scene to arrest him. He was carried off to jail to join Big Rab and Fred, neither of whom had yet been released. 'Defacing Public Property' the police called it.

The number of monkeys in jail was starting to worry Grandpa but no matter what the old silverback said, he just couldn't convince the Big City Police Department to set the monkeys free.

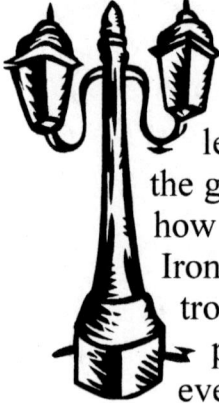

The next monkey to be arrested was called 'The Leaf.' It was a nickname from the jungle. He would leap out of a tree into the air and float to the ground like a leaf. Nobody really knew how he did it but they loved to watch him. Ironically enough, The Leaf got into trouble over a lamp post too. He was out practicing his trick in the street one evening. The only thing he had found that was high enough to jump off were the lamp posts so he climbed up and jumped off every lamp post he came to. The Leaf didn't just get arrested. He was put in a padded cell – 'to protect him from himself.' After all, a monkey who continually jumped off lamp posts was a danger to society and to himself. What if he hurt himself? Or, even worse, what if he landed on someone? At least his padded cell was close to the cells of Fred, Big Rab and Lonely Jake, all of whom were still imprisoned for their crimes.

The ultimate insult to the troop of monkeys came when Grandpa, the old silverback, was arrested by the B.C.T.A. (Big City Tax Authority) for tax evasion. You see, the old man who had taught the monkeys all their manners, airs and graces hadn't told the troop of monkeys anything about taxes. In fact, he hadn't even taught them how to read so Grandpa had just ignored the final demand letters from the B.C.T.A. He didn't really know what a letter was anyway, although he did wonder what these funny pieces of paper were that someone kept giving him each morning.

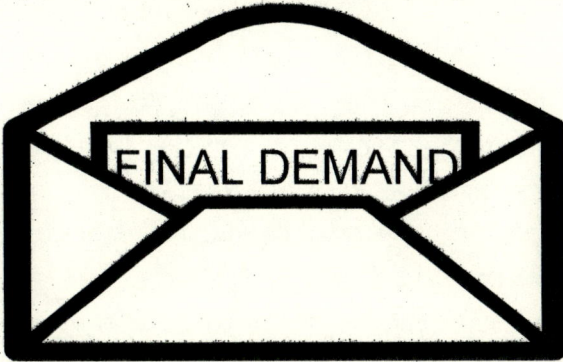

There they all were – the entire troop of monkeys in the jail. Fred was in cell number one for kissing a pretty girl monkey on the street, Big Rab was in cell number two for stealing bananas, Lonely Jake was in cell number three for scratching himself against a lamp post, The Leaf was in cell number four for jumping off lamp posts and Grandpa was in cell number five for not paying his taxes. They really were a sorry little troop of monkeys. Grandpa was starting to regret his decision to bring the monkeys to the big city. Maybe it wasn't such a smart idea after all.

However, the Big City Police Department wasn't completely without compassion. The Police Commissioner knew that they weren't really bad monkeys – they just weren't used to big city life and he had just received a rather odd letter.

Dear Mr. Police Commissioner,

I am writing from the Village At The End Of The World. Until recently, the population of our village was just five people. However, due to unforeseen circumstances, we have had a huge number of people moving to our village. This has included several billion ants, two symphony orchestras, a retired hunter and a very handsome and important lion. As you can imagine, a population of this size now requires some kind of a police force. This is especially important, since both orchestras have a seven member percussion section and drummers are well known to cause more trouble even than monkeys! I hope you will be able to spare some of your police officers to uphold law and order in our village.

Yours faithfully,

Mr. Hubert O. Lion

Mayor,
The Village At The End Of The World

The letter even had a very official looking seal on it, as if to emphasize how important Mr. Hubert Q. Lion really was.

The Police Commissioner's idea was simple. He would send the troop of monkeys to the Village At The End Of The World as their new police force and would solve several problems at one go – the Village At The End Of The World would get their own police force, he would have an empty jail once again and he would stop wasting his time arresting a bunch of very polite but very silly monkeys.

After thinking it over, Grandpa decided that it was the best offer they were going to get – it was better than going back to the jungle and it was definitely better than staying in jail. Grandpa, Fred, Big Rab, Lonely Jake and The Leaf packed their bags and went to the B.C.P.T.A. (Big City Police Training Academy). Since all the other people on the course were human beings, the five monkeys passed the course with flying colors – they were stronger, could run faster and climb better than anyone else and soon they were graduating from the B.C.P.T.A. as policemen (or should that be policemonkeys?). They set out on their journey to the Village At The End Of The

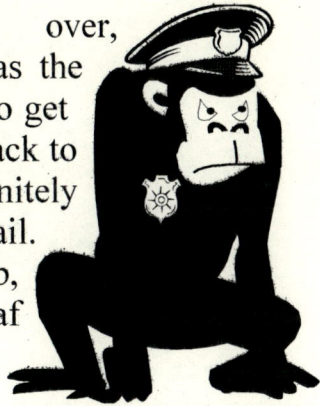

World which, as you know, takes two years to get there.

Grandpa, Fred, Big Rab, Lonely Jake and The Leaf arrived to absolute chaos in the Village At The End Of The World. Of course, there was a welcoming committee made up of the Mayor (Mr. Hubert Q. Lion), the deputy mayor (Wilson), the deputy mayor's daughter (Joy) and the deputy mayor's daughter's fiancée (Bob). When Grandpa produced the letter that the lion had written to the police commissioner to explain who he was, the deputy mayor and his family rolled about laughing – they had never known his real name before. They'd always just called him 'Lion.'

"You're called Hubert Q. Lion?" giggled Wilson.

"What does the Q stand for?" laughed Joy, the deputy mayor's daughter.

"Imagine having a name like that!" guffawed Bob, the deputy mayor's daughter's fiancée.

When they had finally recovered from their laughter, they began to show the troop of monkeys the remains of their once beautiful village. The two symphony orchestras were ruining the whole

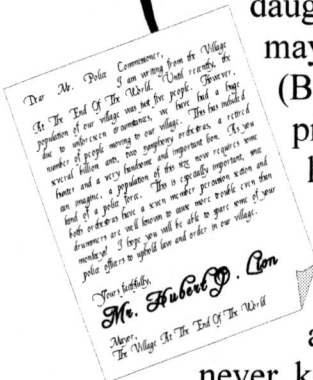

place. Every day, they swam in the ocean. They couldn't even remember the Ten Commandments of the Village At The End Of The World. A couple of violinists had already been lost at sea – probably they fell over the waterfall. The brass section played their trumpets and trombones long into the night, keeping everyone awake. The two men who played the big drums just scared everyone with their strong, hairy arms and their big red faces. As for the ants, it seemed like they made their field bigger every day. The field had become so big that it was soon ready to start eating up the village.

The all new V.A.T.E.O.T.W.P.D. (Village At The End Of The World Police Department) had a job on their hands. It wasn't long before the troop of monkeys had built three new buildings in the village. Each one had big white letters painted on the front.

The first building said V.A.T.E.O.T.W.P.S. (Village At The End Of The World Police Station). The second building said V.A.T.E.O.T.W.C.H. (Village At The End Of The World Court House). The third building said V.A.T.E.O.T.W.C.J. (Village At The End Of The World County Jail). The third building was the biggest building in the whole village. It needed to be with so many drummers running around the place.

Before long, The Leaf was bringing trombonists, violinists, ants and the men who play the big drums into the police station. Lonely Jake would interview them and Fred would charge them. Then they would be taken to the court house where Grandpa was the judge. He would sentence them and they would be taken to prison where Big Rab was the jailor.

Soon, the troop of monkeys had cleaned up the Village At The End Of The World – the percussion sections started behaving themselves, the ants' field suddenly shrank back to its proper size and everyone stopped swimming in the ocean. And that is how the Village At The End Of The World got a troop of monkeys as its police force.

mark mcknight

land of the windmills

Everyone who lived in the Village At The End Of The World had got there by traveling along the Village At The End Of The World Highway. Since they had all been in such a big rush to get there, they hadn't stopped to do any sightseeing along the way. After all, if you knew your journey was going to take two years, you probably wouldn't want to waste any time stopping off to see funny little things along the way. There was, however, one truly remarkable sign about a week before you reached the Village At The End Of The World that aroused everyone's interest. Each person who had seen the sign wanted more than anything else to go and see what it was all about, but they knew they had to keep going on their journey.

The sign was an old piece of wood held to a fence post with a rusty nail. In very untidy handwriting, someone had written in white paint,

'Land Of The Windmills – 2 miles' and underneath there was a big arrow pointing to the right. The sign had obviously been written many years ago and the white paint had faded to a color that could best be described as 'off-cream.' It was the only sign post along the entire Village At The End Of The World Highway. The strange thing was that the sign just seemed to point to nowhere. There was no road that went to the right. There was no cobbled lane that went to the right. There was no dirt track with grass growing in the middle that went to the right. There wasn't any kind of path, track, road, avenue, street or highway. It seemed like the sign pointed to nothing but everyone who had passed by wondered what the sign was all about and what the 'Land Of The Windmills' really was.

Bob and Joy were the two people who were most interested in the Land Of The Windmills. Sometimes, they couldn't sleep at night wondering what it was and how to get there. Other times, they couldn't sleep at night because their orchestras just wouldn't stop playing and the men who played the big drums with the hairy arms and the big red faces were just too loud. When they did fall asleep, they dreamed all kinds of strange dreams about this mysterious place. Most of the rest of the citizens of the Village At

The End Of The World were happy enough but Bob and Joy just couldn't get the Land Of The Windmills out of their heads. It was almost as if the place was calling to them in their dreams.

Have you ever wanted to go to a place that much? I once met a man who wanted more than anything to go to Ireland. So can you guess what he did? He took a holiday there. And that's exactly what Bob and Joy did. They decided they would take a holiday to the Land Of The Windmills. Assuming, that is, they could find it – they knew it would take them one week just to get to the signpost but who knows what might happen after that? Bob and Joy had to make all their plans in absolute secrecy – if they were going on holiday, there was no way they wanted their orchestras to come with them. They didn't tell a soul what they were planning except Wilson, the deputy mayor – he was, after all, Joy's dad.

Soon, all the arrangements were in place. They had packed their bags, bought all the provisions they would need for their journey and got everything ready. In the middle of the night, they both quietly got out of their beds in their own houses and sneaked out, making sure not to wake up any of the orchestra members – if their orchestras came with them, it wouldn't be much

of a holiday. One of the flute players from Bob's orchestra stirred as Bob passed but he just scratched himself, rolled over and fell back asleep. They had done it – Bob and Joy met in the village square and set off on their journey *without* their orchestras.

Of course, when the orchestras awoke the next morning to find Bob and Joy gone, the conductors were furious – they had failed in their jobs. Who was going to provide the soundtrack for their lives now? What were they going to do now that their reason for being in the Village At The End Of The World was gone? They asked around to see if anyone knew what had happened but nobody seemed to know anything. Even Joy's father, the deputy mayor, wasn't giving anything away. There was only one thing to do. If Bob and Joy weren't in the Village At The End Of The World, they could only have gone one direction – along the Village At The End Of The World Highway because nobody was so stupid these days as to swim in the ocean – the Ten Commandments of the Village At The End Of The World were now written on signposts all over the beach so there was no way you could forget them. It took the two orchestras a few days to get ready to go – packing their bags, fixing their instruments and waiting for the men who play the

big drums to be released from jail after they scared some of the cello players. No matter how much the conductors argued with Grandpa, he just wouldn't let them go until they had served their sentence. By the time the two orchestras left the Village At The End Of The World, Bob and Joy were already half way to the Land Of The Windmills.

Eventually, Bob and Joy arrived at the signpost that pointed towards the Land Of The Windmills but now that they were going in the opposite direction, things looked very different indeed. There was a huge, brand new sign post with lights and everything that said, 'Land Of The Windmills – 2 miles' and underneath there was a big white arrow pointing to the left. There was a huge road that turned off to the left – a big, brand new road with street lights and all kinds of nice things.

Bob didn't think this could be right – when he had been going towards the Village At The End Of The World, he had just seen and old hand painted sign pointing to nothing. Now that he was coming from the Village At The End Of The World, there was a huge, brand new sign post pointing along a major highway. Bob walked on past the signpost and the road and turned around

to pretend he was coming the other way. He saw the old hand painted sign pointing to nothing. He turned around and pretended to be walking the other way again and saw the new signpost and the big road again. Well, that was certainly a very weird thing – a road that you could only see when you were going one direction but not the other. Bob and Joy had never seen something like that before.

Bob and Joy had to be among the first people to travel along this road – after all, you could only see it when you were coming from the Village At The End Of The World and, as far as we know, Bob and Joy were the first people ever to travel that direction along the Village At The End Of The World Highway – everyone else had simply stayed put in the Village At The End Of The World. In just two miles, they would come to the end of their journey and find out exactly what the Land Of The Windmills really was. Bob and Joy were so excited to finally reach their destination.

Bob and Joy were on their holidays – they had been taking their time on the journey. They had stopped for picnics in fields full of sunflowers. They had picked blackberries from the side of the road. Just as Bob and Joy turned off the Village At The End Of The World

Highway onto Land Of The Windmills Boulevard, they heard music in the distance – the orchestras were practicing as they travelled. It was only then that they realised the orchestras were following them, and they had almost caught up since Bob and Joy had wasted so much time on their journey. All of a sudden, the Land Of The Windmills wasn't so much somewhere to go on holidays as somewhere to hide from the orchestras.

Land Of The Windmills Boulevard climbed up and up into the mountains. Soon, the road curved around the crest of a ridge and Bob and Joy saw what they had traveled so long to view – the Land Of The Windmills in all its glory. Thousands and thousands of brightly painted windmills were all over the banks and floor of a long, shallow valley. Each one was perpetually turning in unison with the rest. Each windmill was a different colour from the rest. There weren't just red windmills: there were scarlet, rust and cherry windmills. There weren't just yellow windmills: there were ochre, lemon and sunflower windmills. There weren't just green windmills: there were emerald, lime and jade windmills. There weren't just blue windmills: there were indigo, aquamarine and turquoise windmills. It

was the most beautiful thing that Bob and Joy had ever seen. All along the valley there were thousands and thousands of these windmills, all gently turning in the breeze.

Suddenly, the journey to get here all seemed worthwhile, just to see this one beautiful scene looking along the valley at these windmills. The road wound its way down the side of the valley and along the floor of the valley. Once Bob and Joy had caught their breath after this breathtaking view, they decided they would follow the road – after all, they didn't want the two orchestras to catch up with them.

As they walked along the road, they noticed something very odd – the entire time they had been in the Land Of The Windmills, they hadn't seen a single person. All of these windmills seemed to be here in the middle of nowhere with no-one to look after them. However, as they walked along the road, they soon bumped into a very old man who carried a little oil can. He introduced himself as the caretaker of the Land Of The Windmills. He explained that he was the only person who lived here and he'd been hoping that someone would come along to keep him company. He had even put up a big sign on the Village At The End Of The Road Highway but so far, Bob and Joy were the only ones who had

mark mcknight

come along. It wasn't long before Bob, Joy and the old man were sitting at a table in one of the windmills with a pot of tea on the stove and some pancakes on the griddle.

The old man told Bob and Joy all about the Land Of The Windmills. Bob and Joy told the old man all about the Village At The End Of The World, about Mr. Hubert Q. Lion, the mayor, about Wilson, the deputy mayor and Joy's father who's main job was to brush the lion's teeth, about the ants, about the monkeys who were policemen and about the two symphony orchestras who were, at that very moment, standing on Land Of The Windmills Boulevard at the edge of the valley, marveling at the beautiful sight of thousands and thousands of multi-colored windmills that lay before them.

"I should very much like to visit your Village At The End Of The World," said the old man, "but I can't leave the Land Of The Windmills – each windmill needs to be given two drops of oil every day. Otherwise, they will stop turning and a Land Of The Broken Windmills wouldn't be nearly so beautiful."

It wasn't long before Bob had hatched a plan where the old man wouldn't just be able to visit the Village At The End Of The World, he

would actually be able to retire from his job as caretaker of the Land Of The Windmills and go to live with his new found friends. Bob, Joy and the old man went to the very far end of the valley to the very last two windmills. One was powder blue and the other was baby pink. They lit a fire in the fireplace of each one, went out the back door and climbed back out of the valley through the fields instead of along the road. That way, they were able to get behind the two symphony orchestras again to get back to the Village At The End Of The World Highway without the conductors seeing them. And so Bob, Joy and the old man began the journey back to the Village At The End Of The World while the two orchestras were still in the Land Of The Windmills looking for them.

When the conductors saw smoke coming from the chimneys of the two windmills at the end of the valley, they went straight there. One orchestra went to the powder blue windmill on the left hand side of the road. The other went to the baby pink windmill on the right hand side of the road. They assumed that they were about to find Bob and Joy, so they got ready to resume the soundtracks for their lives. The violinists raised their bows, the brass section took a deep breath ready to play and the men who played the big

drums got their drum sticks ready but as the conductors burst through the doors of each windmill, they found the same letter on both kitchen tables…

To Mr. Conductor,

Welcome to the Land Of The Windmills. You, and your orchestra, are now the off-icial caretakers. Each windmill needs two drops of oil every day or they will stop turning. This would be simply awful as a Land Of The Broken Windmills is not nearly so beautiful. You will find an oil-can on the table.

Yours sincerely,

Pete

Former Caretaker.

Land Of The Windmills

P.T.O.

The note continued on the other side...

P.S. I met your friends, Bob and Joy. I'm retiring to the Village At The End Of The World. They say I can live with them there.

The orchestras had taken it upon themselves to start an appropriate piece of music for this moment. That just made the conductors even angrier – Bob and Joy had gotten away from them not just once, but twice. The conductors sat down to work out what they were going to do. This was a very big problem indeed. Eventually, the man who played the big drum with the hairy arms and the big, red face from Joy's orchestra came up with an idea.

"We don't all have to stay, do we?" asked the man. "I mean, if one man was doing it by himself for all these years, we could just leave one orchestra to be the caretakers. They would be able to oil all the windmills in a fraction of the time and they would be able to spend the rest of their time practicing. The other orchestra could go back to the Village At The End Of The World and just play music for the whole village. It's been getting a bit boring just playing music for one person anyway, especially since they keep running off on us. Then we could change places

once a year – the orchestra that was in the Village At The End Of The World would come to the Land Of The Windmills and vice versa. We could even do a very big, special joint concert in the Land Of The Windmills every year. People might even come from the Big City to hear us."

Everyone agreed that the man who played the big drum with the hairy arms and the big, red face was a genius. It was an excellent idea. They drew straws to see who would stay and who would go. Joy's orchestra drew the short straw so they had to stay. The two orchestras said their goodbyes and Bob's orchestra set off on their journey back to the Village At The End Of The World.

Now that the Village At The End Of The World only had one symphony orchestra, things got a lot more peaceful – there weren't so many percussion players running about causing trouble. The monkeys even started working only in the mornings since there was so little police work to do. For now, life was good in the Village At The End Of The World. For now…

the giant's dessert

I'm sure that by now, you know that very strange things can happen in the Village At The End Of The World – they are bound to when you have a lion for mayor and a troop of monkeys for your police force.

However, on this one day, something extra strange happened. We haven't really heard much about the original five people who lived in the Village At The End Of The World before the lion arrived. This story is about the little baby that the lion ended up rescuing instead of eating when he arrived.

The baby's name was Sara but everyone called her Chihuahua because she was very small and she liked to talk a whole lot! She was like a little chihuahua dog that was always running around and making noise so everyone called her Chihuahua. By now, Chihuahua was really starting to grow up very big and strong. She would go hunting with her bow and arrow and she would help the symphony orchestras when they were trying to build their houses.

Chihuahua was like most little children – she had what they call a 'sweet tooth.' She loved to eat anything that was sweet. When she was awake, she was thinking about doughnuts. When she was asleep, she was dreaming about cakes. When she got some money, she spent it on candy. She would do anything to get her hands on ice-cream and cookies. When she drank a cup of tea, she put seven spoons full of sugar in it. Seven! Instead of orange juice at breakfast, she drank sweet lemonade. Instead of a sandwich for lunch, she ate a candy bar. It was a disaster for Chihuahua if there was no dessert after dinner.

At that time, there was only one map of the Village At The End Of The World which hung in the mayor's office. In fact, it's the same map that is on the very first page of this book. It had been very carefully drawn in pencil by one of the original residents of the village and presented to the mayor when he had taken up office. Unfortunately, whoever had drawn the map wasn't particularly good at spelling. As a result, there were all kinds of mistakes on the map.

Being such a small village, the residents regularly visited each other and on this particular day, Chihuahua was visiting the mayor in his office. While Mr. Hubert Q. Lion was making some tea, Chihuahua was looking at the map hanging on the wall in the mayor's office. Imagine Chihuahua's surprise when she found a huge area on the map that was marked 'Giant's Dessert.' Well this was something entirely new to Chihuahua. Giant's Dessert could mean only one thing – there was a dessert so big that only a giant would be able to eat it. Chihuahua simply had to go and see this Giant's Dessert. She wondered what it might be – ice-cream or maybe a huge apple pie? Would there be a giant there eating it?

Chihuahua quickly got a piece of paper and a pen and copied down the map so that she would know how to get there. It was quite simple, really. Just follow Village At The End Of The World Highway for one week, turn left onto Land Of The Windmills Boulevard, pass right through the Land Of The Windmills and as soon as you pass the last windmill and climb out of the valley again, you're right there in the Giant's Dessert.

Chihuahua didn't even wait to drink the tea that the mayor was making for her. She quickly wrote a note on the mayor's desk…

bear mr. lion,

   I've gone to the dessert.
Thanks for the tea.

love from

   chihuahua.

With that, she ran home, packed her bags and set off for the Giant's Dessert.

   It took a long time before anyone worked out what was really going on. To begin with, the mayor thought that Chihuahua had gone home for dessert. 'Humph, nice of her to invite me,' he thought but soon Chihuahua's mother came around to see if Mr. Hubert Q. Lion knew where she was – Chihuahua hadn't come home. The mayor and Chihuahua's mother went to find the monkeys to see if the police could help them. Having cleaned up the village, the monkeys didn't have much to do so Grandpa, Fred, Big Rab, Lonely Jake and The Leaf immediately jumped on this case. They had been looking for some official police business to keep them occupied anyway – they were getting tired of playing cards in the police station.

The first thing they did was to go to the mayor's office to see if they could work out where she had gone and what had made her leave so suddenly. The Leaf, who was really the brains behind the police force, was studying the mayor's desk to see if there were any clues when he saw the notebook. He suddenly realized that if he held the top sheet up to the light, he could see an imprint of what had been written on the previous sheet. It wasn't long before he had traced the outline of the map that Chihuahua had drawn. You and I know that it was the map but Mr. Hubert Q. Lion, Chihuahua's mother and the monkeys didn't work it out straight away. There were no words written on the map – just five little huts in a circle beside the ocean and a road which turned left, went past a windmill and straight into a huge ice cream.

The Leaf was almost ready to give up trying to work out what it all meant when he caught a glimpse of the map hanging on the wall out of the corner of his eye. Suddenly, it all made sense. The five little huts beside the ocean were the Village At The End Of The World, the windmill was the Land Of The Windmills and the huge ice cream was the Giant's Dessert. The Leaf still wasn't sure what it all meant but he explained it to

the rest of the monkeys, Mr. Hubert Q. Lion and
Chihuahua's mother.

Grandpa, Fred, Big Rab, Lonely Jake and
Mr. Hubert Q. Lion didn't know what it meant
either but Chihuahua's mother knew…
"My baby has gone to the Giant's Dessert," she
said. "She's always had a sweet tooth and she
must have seen it on the map and decided she
wanted to go there. My poor little girl. What will
she do all alone? I mean, there must be plenty to
eat in the Giant's Dessert but what about the
giants?"

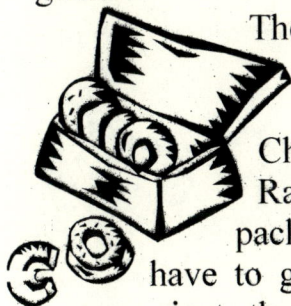

The Leaf quickly went into action.
Grandpa and Mr. Hubert Q.
Lion were left to comfort
Chihuahua's mother. Fred and Big
Rab were dispatched to start
packing – someone was going to
have to go after Chihuahua and if there
were giants there, Big Rab should be the one to
go. After all, if the The Leaf was the brains of the
operation, Big Rab was certainly the brawn.
Lonely Jake was sent to find out who drew the
map to see if they could find out anything more.
The Leaf decided to make some tea.

It wasn't long before everyone arrived back
at the mayor's office. Fred and Big Rab were
ready to leave at a moment's notice – they were
like a two-man (or a two monkey) rapid reaction
force. Lonely Jake arrived with the man who had

drawn the map. Grandpa explained the situation to Cyril the cartographer (for that is what you call someone who draws maps) as plainly as he could. He too was ope of the original residents of the Village At The End Of The World.

"Why would anyone want to go to the desert?" asked Cyril.

"She has a sweet tooth," said Chihuahua's mother, "and she probably just wanted to eat some of the dessert."

"What on earth are you talking about?" asked Cyril. "There's nothing to eat in the desert – it's just sand, sand and more sand. For miles and miles and miles. There's sand everywhere and nothing else."

Suddenly, as if someone had flicked a switch in everyone's mind, each person in the room came to the realization of what a horrible mistake had been made. Mr. Hubert Q. Lion, Cyril the cartographer, Grandpa, Fred, Big Rab, Lonely Jake, The Leaf and Chihuahua's mother at the same instant knew exactly what had happened. Cyril's spelling had been so poor that when he had drawn the map many years ago, before the lion had even arrived in the Village At The End Of The World, instead of writing Giant's Desert, he had written Giant's

Dessert. Because of his horrid mistake, a little girl was, right now, trekking into the middle of a desert by herself, with no food and expecting to find a giant ice cream. She wasn't expecting the ice cream to be sand flavoured!

The Leaf had to change his plans for a start. Fred and Big Rab weren't ready to go off into the desert. They had been planning on going to the dessert. The desert was a whole different thing. It was called the Giant's Desert because it was so big, not because there were any giants there. It would be like trying to find a needle in a haystack. Once again, Grandpa and Mr. Hubert Q. Lion stayed to comfort Chihuahua's mother. Fred and Big Rab were once again sent home to repack for their journey. Cyril the cartographer was informed that he too would be making the journey – he would know where to go and he needed to make amends for his big mistake. Lonely Jake was sent to get some biscuits and once again, The Leaf made some tea. It wasn't long before all eight people and animals were again gathered in the mayor's office making their final preparations. The Leaf and Lonely Jake would remain in the Village At The End Of The World to maintain law and order – they couldn't just all up and leave at once. Grandpa would be in charge of comforting Chihuahua's mother until the young girl was

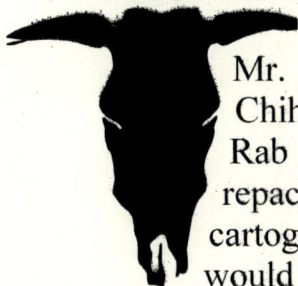

safely returned. Mr. Hubert Q. Lion, as mayor, obviously had to stay put. That left Fred, Big Rab and Cyril the cartographer to set off in search of Chihuahua.

Speaking of Chihuahua, I'm sure you're wondering how she was getting on in the desert all by herself. Chihuahua followed her directions to the letter: travel along Village At The End Of The World Highway for one week, turn left onto Land Of The Windmills Boulevard and keep going. In the Land Of The Windmills, Chihuahua had stopped for tea with Joy's orchestra who were still performing their duties as caretakers of the Land Of The Windmills. Luckily for Chihuahua, there were all kinds of sweet things there – sweetbread, cakes, doughnuts, pastries, éclairs and croissants. It was lucky for Chihuahua, because although she didn't yet realise it, this would be her last meal for a while. After filling herself up on tea and pastries in front of the conductor and a few violinists, Chihuahua once again got back on the road. At least she didn't have to see the man who played the big drum with his hairy arms and his big, red face – he really scared poor little Chihuahua.

Once Chihuahua passed the powder blue and baby pink windmills right at the end of the valley, she knew she was about to arrive in the Giant's Dessert. Chihuahua couldn't wait to find out what it really was. This was the moment she had been waiting for. She climbed out of the valley, leaving the Land Of The Windmills behind her, and was instantly greeted by a huge expanse of sand dunes. As far as the eye could see there was sand stretching in every direction. Except behind her, of course – that's where the Land Of The Windmills was!

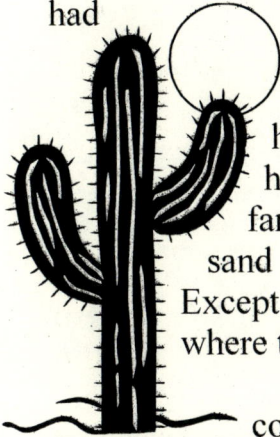

To begin with, Chihuahua was confused by the lack of dessert and the abundance of sand. 'What happened to the Giant's Dessert?' she wondered. She quickly decided that all the sand was just around the edge of the Giant's Dessert to protect if from people coming in to eat. But Chihuahua wasn't just a normal person - she had once almost been eaten by a lion and had almost fallen off the end of the world. No, Chihuahua was not going to be discouraged by a little bit of sand. This was a great prize and a sand dune was not going to stand between Chihuahua and the Giant's Dessert.

After many hours of trekking in the desert, trying beyond all hope to find the Giant's Dessert, Chihuahua was hungry, lonely and afraid but most of all she was thirsty. All she wanted was a little cup of water.

Fortunately, Fred, Big Rab and Cyril the cartographer had found Chihuahua's footprints in the sand and were following them. By the time they had caught up with Chihuahua, the poor girl was about to collapse from thirst. Luckily, Fred had brought some extra water along with him that he gave to Chihuahua. It took them a while to convince Chihuahua that there had been a mistake on the map and that it was the Giant's Desert and not the Giant's Dessert.

Big Rab lifted Chihuahua onto his back and the little group trekked back out of the desert, through the Land Of The Windmills and back to the Village At The End Of The World. Chihuahua's mother was so happy to see her that she forgot to tell her daughter off and The Leaf soon served tea and cookies for everyone. The next day, Mr. Hubert Q. Lion made Cyril the cartographer draw a new map and checked the spelling personally to make sure that something like this would never happen again. As for Chihuahua, she still had her sweet tooth but she never again ran off without first checking with her mother.

the men who play the big drums

The men who played the big drums always seemed to be getting into trouble. It wasn't that they meant to, it was just that they looked so scary that it always caused problems. For a start, they had big, hairy arms. When you saw their big, hairy arms, you thought they were going to grab you and throw you into the sea. Yes sir, those were some big, hairy arms. For a second thing, they had big red faces. Have you ever seen someone play the bagpipes? Or someone who doesn't like to run around much? The men who played the big drums always had big, red faces as if they had been running way too much. Or maybe they'd exhausted themselves by throwing too many people into the sea. Aside from all of that, the thing that really scared everyone was this: the men who played the big drums were loud. And when I say loud, I mean LOUD!!!

The problem was that the men who played the big drums were used to playing their big drums as loud as they could and with their big, strong, hairy arms, when they played as loud as they could it was very loud indeed. As a result, the men who played the big drums were now almost deaf after a lifetime of playing their big drums so loud. They were so deaf that most of the time they couldn't hear the rest of the orchestra, so it was just luck whether or not they would actually be playing the same piece of music. Most of the time, they just played what they felt like playing.

The biggest problem with these men was when they started practicing. The violins and the flutes and the trumpets would practice every day to make sure that they were still good but hitting the big drum isn't exactly very difficult. It was usually about once a week that the men who played the big drums got around to doing a bit of practice and when they practiced, boy did it cause BIG problems.

mark mcknight

When the men who played the big drums started practicing, all kinds of things could happen. Once the people and animals who lived in the Village At The End Of The World heard the first beat of the drums, they knew it was time for urgent action, otherwise all kinds of crazy things might befall them.

For a start, everyone knew that the first thing they had to do was to block up their ears with something otherwise, they would probably go deaf. In those days, there was no such thing as foam ear plugs so you just had to stop your ears up with whatever you could find.

Mr. Hubert Q. Lion was sitting in his office one day when he heard the first beat of the drums. He quickly grabbed a cheese sandwich and an old sock and put one in each ear. He decided to have a walk through the village to make sure that everyone was fine – after all, many strange things happened when the drums were beating. The first people he met were Chihuahua and her mother. Chihuahua had a carrot sticking out of one ear and a potato in the other. Her mother had found two nicely shaped rocks to shut out the sound. Mr. Hubert Q. Lion tried to stop to talk but since everyone's ears were blocked, he eventually gave up and kept on walking. Next, Mr. Lion met the entire Village At The End Of The

World Police Department – Grandpa, Big Rab, The Leaf, Fred and Lonely Jake. They all had their fingers in each other's ears – it was a very funny sight to see five monkeys walking along holding each other's ears. Mr. Lion laughed so much that the cheese sandwich fell out of his ear and Big Rab ran over, picked it up and started to eat it before the lion knew what was going on. Fortunately, Mr. Hubert Q. Lion was able to wrestle it back off Big Rab and put it back in his ear before he had to listen to any more of the drumming. Everyone the lion met on the street had their ears stuffed with all kinds of strange things: fruit, vegetables, old clothes, dead fish and anything, in fact, that would shut out the incredible noise of the men who played the big drums practicing.

Once you had blocked your ears up, that wasn't the problem finished with. You see, when the men who played the big drums started practicing, it was something like a very long, slow earthquake. It was so loud that it actually made people's houses shake. When you heard the drums and you had finished stuffing your ears, the next thing you did was to run home to make sure everything was still OK. You had to make sure that your cups didn't fall off the shelf, you had to make sure that your pictures didn't fall

off the wall and most importantly, you had to make sure that your house didn't fall over. Not that you could do much about it if your house was going to fall over but at least you could make sure that your cups didn't fall of the shelf and that your pictures didn't fall off the wall.

Luckily for the residents of the Village At The End Of The World, they would usually only have to put up with one of the drummers at a time – the other would be with his orchestra in the Land Of The Windmills as they took their turn as caretakers. That at least brought the noise level down to an acceptable level. The problem came once every year when the two orchestras were preparing for their annual concert in the Land Of The Windmills because that is when both orchestras and more importantly both of the men who played the big drums would have to play at the same time.

'The Greatest Concert In The World,' as it had come to be known, was one of the most important occasions on the social calendar in the big city. With the recent invention of the steam train, the B.C.R.C. (Big City Railroad Corporation) had build a train track right through the Giant's Desert to bring people to the concert each year. The train could make the journey from the Big City to the Land of the Windmills   in

about a day and a half. What the concert goers didn't realise was that they could have been in the Village At The End Of The World in just a week: travel all the way along Land Of The Windmills Boulevard, turn right at the end onto Village At The End Of The World Highway and in a week's time you would be there. However, none of the audience had ever made the trip and none of the residents of the Village At The End Of The World had gone the opposite direction either – they were happy where they were. Anyway, the trains only ran once a year to bring people to and from the concert.

Each year, for two weeks before the concert, Pete (the retired caretaker) would return to the Land of the Windmills to oil the windmills so that both orchestras could return to the Village At The End Of The World for two weeks of intensive rehearsals before the great concert. That is when the problems arose because that is when the two men who play the big drums with the hairy arms and the big, red faces would be playing at the same time. Twice the drums meant twice the noise.

Each year, before the rehearsals began, the two conductors would meet together to try to find a solution to the men who play the big drums with the hairy arms and the big, red faces.

They had tried all kinds of solutions. One year, they had decided that instead of giving the men drumsticks, they would give them breadsticks. Interestingly, this had made the men much quieter in their drumming but they just became too annoying when they kept asking for some dip for their breadsticks. Another year they had given the men pillows instead of drums. To begin with, this had worked just fine until the men who played the big drums had hit the pillows so hard that they had exploded. There were feathers everywhere!

This year, however, the conductors were entirely out of ideas. They simply had no idea what they were going to do about the problem of the men who played the big drums with the hairy arms and the big, red faces. They thought and thought but they had no ideas left. They even talked to the mayor (Mr. Hubert Q. Lion), the deputy mayor (Wilson) and the chief of police (Grandpa), none of whom had any ideas either.

The musicians in the rest of the two orchestras were beginning to complain too – they were starting to go deaf from all of the noise that the men who played the big drums were making. A solution had to be found and fast!

There is one original resident of the Village At The End Of The World that we have but met in passing and it is he who was the

one to come up with the eventual solution although it came in a round about way. Baz was the father to Chihuahua, husband to Chihuahua's mother and son to the little old lady who made such a fuss over the ants moving in to the Village At The End Of The World.

Baz was something of an inventor: he was always tinkering, taking things apart, putting them back together and generally fixing things, making things and getting almost everything to work a little better. There were no gadgets or gizmos in the village that had not been designed, built or modified by Baz.

The conductors, tired of the noise from the men who played the big drums eventually decided that they would talk to Baz to see if he could invent something that would solve this problem. Baz immediately set his mind to this seemingly insurmountable problem. He thought and thought and thought and thought but he could think of no way around it. He went to some rehearsals to watch and listen to the men who played the big drums and to see if he could have any ideas. He drew pictures on his blackboard, he wrote down mathematical formulas and complicated scientific data but each time, he reached that same conclusion: the men who played the big drums with the hairy arms and the big, red

faces were too loud. That was all he could come up with no matter what way he looked at it. He couldn't work out exactly how to solve this most complex of problems.

For the whole fist week of rehearsals, Baz just couldn't think of anything he could invent or make or fix to get around this difficulty but then, at the end of the first week, Baz woke up in the middle of the night in a cold sweat. He had had a dream about something that was worth a try. He wasn't sure but it was crazy enough that it might just work.

Immediately, he jumped out of work and ran to the conductors' houses and explained his idea. The first conductor was understandably dubious. He thought it was a mad-cap scheme that would never work. The second conductor on the other hand could see the spark of inspiration that might be enough to make this concert a success.

This would take all of Baz's knowledge and skill and there was just about enough time to build it before the concert in seven days' time. Baz began work straight away – he would have to work around the clock to get everything done that he needed.

The first thing he did, in the middle of the night was to run around the village collecting

everything he needed – wires, electrical components, batteries, old bits of scrap metal, a spot welder, a plumber's tool kit, several old tires, a hair dryer, some rotten vegetables, a teapot, two hundred dessert forks, 100ft of razor wire, a bar of soap, a sharp knife and as much sand as the monkeys could carry.

   To begin with, the residents of the Village At The End Of The World were not impressed – Baz was running around in the middle of the night making all kinds of noise, asking to borrow all kinds of weird things but as soon as they found out what it was for, they all offered their unquestioning assistance. If there was anything they could do to help, they were willing even if it was the middle of the night.

   Baz set up his makeshift workshop in the middle of the village green and set to work. It was now 3:00am and the noise he was making was almost as bad as the noise that comes from the men who played the big drums! By daybreak, there was a pile of sand taller than a house that the monkeys had carried from the beach. There were bits of stuff everywhere – it was like an explosion in a scrap yard but Baz didn't look up from his work once. He tinkered and hammered and welded like a man possessed. He knew that it would be a challenge to build one of his inventions

mark mcknight

by the end of the week but to build two in time for the concert, well that would be something else entirely.

During the day, people came to watch Baz at his work – they were fascinated at how someone could work so hard. By Thursday, Baz hadn't eaten or slept in four days, the concert was in another two days and his invention still wasn't finished. The pile of sand had disappeared, along with the tires, the two hundred forks and the razor wire. Where they had gone, nobody was quite sure but at least the village square looked a little tidier. Baz's work seemed to have changed too. In the beginning, there had been a lot of noise, particular a lot of hammering. Now Baz seemed to be working on something very small. So small that you could only see it if you went right up close to it. Yet he still worked just as frantically to finish his invention.

For those watching, the time ticked by painfully slowly – it always did for the couple of days before the concert. For Baz, the clock whizzed around so quickly that it spurred him on to work even harder.

Soon, the orchestras were packing up to travel to the Land Of The Windmills for the concert and Baz still wasn't finished his invention. If anything, it was even smaller now but he still worked with

111

the same drive to finish it. The orchestra had to depart without him – Baz hoped he would be able to catch them up if he finished on time.

Two hours after the orchestra had departed, Baz looked up for the first time in a week with a triumphant gleam in his eye. Quick as a flash, he dropped the two tiny little somethings into a black velvet bag and set off along the Village At The End Of The World Highway in pursuit of the two symphony orchestras, hoping that he would arrive in the Land Of The Windmills before the concert had started.

Unfortunately, the orchestras were also traveling with the same fury – they were also late and didn't want to miss their own concert. By the time Baz reached the turn off for Land Of The Windmills Boulevard, he knew the orchestra were well ahead of him. As he came over the crest into the Land Of The Windmills, he could see both orchestras on stage at the other end of the valley tuning up for the start of the concert, just between the powder blue and baby pink windmills that were the last two in the valley. The valley was packed. This year, thousands off people had come from the Big City to hear the concert. In fact, the Big City Railroad Corporation had laid on extra trains, since there were so many people who wanted to come.

With a renewed fire in his belly, Baz set off to reach the stage before the concert began. He ran like the wind and arrived behind the stage just as the two conductors were introducing the concert. As the conductor raised his baton to begin the first piece, Baz sneaked up behind the men who play the big drums with the hairy arms and the big, red faces and slipped something very small into each of their right ears.

The concert began and it was a triumph. Every member of the orchestra played their heart out, including the men who play the big drums with the hairy arms and the big, red faces and they didn't even play too loud. For the first time, they even played along with the rest of the orchestra. It turned out that the men who played the big drums were so deaf that they couldn't even hear their own drums. The reason that they played so loudly was so that they could feel the vibration from their drums. Baz had invented a hearing aid for each of them so not only could they hear their own drums, they could also hear the rest of the orchestra. It made such a difference that when the newspapers in the Big City reviewed the concert, they all mentioned how excellent the men who played the big drums with the hairy arms and the big, red faces had been.

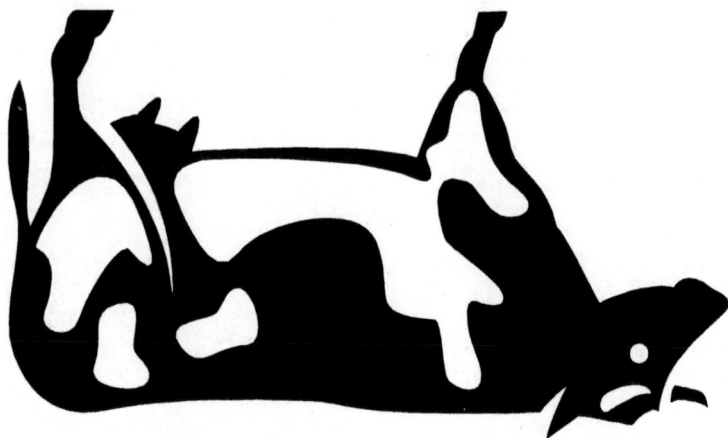

what's wrong with these cows?

With all of the extra land around the Village At The End Of The World, it seems only natural that some of the residents would get into agriculture as a means of passing the time. Interestingly enough, it was the violinists that took farming to heart and really made a go of it. Although the land wasn't great for growing crops, there was some fantastic pasture land between the Village At The End Of The World and the Land Of The Windmills so the violinists decided to form a dairy farming co-operative. They began by selling their milk to the residents of the Village At The End Of The World but soon they expanded

114

their operation and began transporting milk for sale to the Big City in refrigerated trains along the railway that the Big City Railroad Corporation had built to bring people to the annual 'Greatest Concert In The World.'

For a time, the V.D.C. (Violinists' Dairy Co-Operative) was a roaring success. The pristine pasturelands and the easy life of the cows meant that the milk was some of the best in the known world. Quite soon, the violinists had become experts in everything to do with cattle. They even had a few 'cow vets' who were, of course, self trained but who seemed to know everything about what might be wrong with a sick cow and just the right thing to do or say to make poor Daisy feel better.

Unfortunately, this success was to come to an end suddenly and unexpectedly in a way that no-one could have predicted. Every morning, the violinists would go out to the pastures and bring all the cows back to the Village At The End Of The World to milk them. Thousands and thousands of cows would pass through the village every morning to be milked but no-one outside the co-operative was quite sure how so few people milked so many cows . This was always, however, a very closely guarded secrets – one that even the violists (viola players) were not party to.

When a cow goes to sleep, it sleeps standing up. It can't lie down like you or I which is a shame but if you're a cow, you probably don't know any better. Yet one morning when the violinists went out to the fields to bring the cattle back to the village for milking, they discovered that there was a very big problem. Instead of finding all of the cows standing up like they were every morning, every cow was lying on its back with four legs pointing straight up in the air. The cows seemed happy enough in this position and were merrily chewing the cud but it obviously presented problems in that they would be unable to walk to the village to be milked. There was only one thing for it: the violinists would have to milk the cows the old fashioned way: with a bucket. Even though the cows were upside down, there was nothing to be done – the co-operative had quotas to meet and delivery schedules that must be kept.

So despite the inconvenience of it all, the violinists returned to the fields with their buckets to milk the cows one by one. Despite the problems of milking an upside down cow, it wasn't long before the violinists were carrying buckets of rich creamy milk back to the village to be bottled and shipped to the Big City.

If you have ever looked carefully at a bottle of milk, you will know that the cream (the best part) always rises to the top of the bottle but as the violinists bottled the milk from the upside down cows, they realized that something was very seriously wrong. The cream was sinking to the bottom instead of rising to the top. Not only were the cows upside down, they were producing upside down milk. This was not just a minor problem of milk. What about all the things that milk was used to make. Porridge? Milkshakes? The thought of an upside down cup of tea just filled the heart with dread. This was a major crisis for the Violinists' Dairy Co-Operative and for dairy farmers in general.

The Cow Vets were called immediately (a couple of violinists who knew about every cow disease under the sun). They had encountered some strange cow diseases in their time: Backwards Cow Disease that could only be cured by singing and a really odd one that made the cows float eighteen inches (approximately) above the ground. They had never seen anything like this. This 'Upside Down Cow Disease' was something new to them entirely. They simply couldn't understand it. There was nothing that they knew of which would cause this and there was certainly nothing that they knew of that would cure it. The problem with the milk, they had to assume, would fix itself if the cows were cured of their problem.

What was to be done? Village officials were consulted (the mayor, the deputy mayor and the police chief). They too had no idea how to go about solving this problem. Eventually, the boss of the Violinists' Dairy Co-Operative began pulling his own hair out and ran into the streets screaming, "WHAT'S WRONG WITH THESE COWS? WHAT'S WRONG WITH THESE COWS?"

Taking charge, the mayor (Mr. Hubert Q. Lion) decided that the Cow Vets should travel on the milk train to the Big City to see if they could find an expert who would know what was wrong with these cows. After all, upside down milk would not help the reputation of the Village At The End Of The World. The cow vets packed their bags, said their farewells and set off to the Big City with the

knowledge that they were the only hope for the Violinists' Dairy Co-Operative.

Unfortunately, while they were away, the upside down cows still needed milking so every day the violinists would return to the fields with their buckets to get some more upside down milk. The upside down milk was piling up in the village – everyone was too scared to use it for fear of what might happen. There was even a rumour going around that if you drank upside down milk then you too would find yourself upside down – standing on your head with your feet sticking up in the air.

The cow vets searched and searched in the Big City to try to find someone who would know something about their problem. They asked all kinds of vets, farmers, experts, teachers, doctors, nurses, politicians, lawyers and even a man who trained donkeys to do tricks. In fact, everyone they met was asked if they knew anything about upside down cows. Sadly, no-one knew a thing about it and some people were so rude as to laugh in their faces. They said, "Don't be so silly! How can there be such a thing as Upside Down Cow Disease. The mere idea of upside down milk is simply preposterous."

They had almost given up hope of ever finding anyone who knew anything about upside down cow disease when one old, old man they spoke to half remembered something that had happened to him years before. He had met a farmer at a crossroads once who kept losing his animals. He remembered that there had been something funny happened with some cows. Maybe the cow vets should go and talk to him. The crossroads was just outside the Big City and, believe it or not, was in the exact centre of the world.

Meanwhile, back in the Village At The End Of The World, thing were getting desperate. Even the ants didn't want the upside down milk and usually they would eat anything at all, particularly if it was free! The violinists had run out of buckets to collect the upside down milk so now they were using whatever they could find: vases, flower pots, soup bowls, watering cans. In fact, anything that could possibly be used for the milking was being used.

The cow vets rushed to the crossroads to see if they could find this farmer. Was he still alive? Did he know anything about Upside Down Cow Disease? Why did he keep losing his animals? The two cow vets arrived at the crossroads and there they found the same farmer that Wilson had met many years before with just a few more grey hairs and a few more wrinkles. As they explained their problem, the old farmer began to tell them a story...

"Many years ago, an old hunter came through here looking for t' Village At T' End Of T' World. Now to be sure, oi made some mistakes and oi sent him t' wrong way once or twice but he did 'elp me find moi sheep and moi goats and moi pigs. He did refuse t' 'elp find moi cows, though. Now strange as that was, in t' end when oi found moi cows, they were all there upside down in t' field. And you'll never guess wha'...they were all giving upside down milk."

The two cow vets were beside themselves – finally they had found someone who knew what he was talking about, even if he was a little eccentric. They both began asking questions at once: what did you do? How did you cure them? Were the cows OK? Did their milk go back to normal? The farmer held up his hands to hush them and said, "Well, oi'll tell ye but first ye must help me find moi chickens." The two cow vets groaned but it was clear that they would have to help this man before they got any information.

They began the search for the missing chickens and it wasn't long before they heard the unmistakable 'cluck, cluck' and more importantly

smelled the smell of a brood of chickens and so the farmer resumed his story...

"Well, oi talked to all kinds of experts about moi upside down cows and best we could figure, moi cows had gone on strike. They wanted better pay and conditions – a day off from milking in the week and a few sugar lumps every now and then as a treat. Oh, and to make sure that the people who were milking them didn't have cold hands. They didn't like that!"

The two cow vets looked at each other, then at the farmer and then at the chickens. The chickens were doing something very odd – instead of sitting down to lay their eggs, they would fly up into the air and lay their egg so that it smashed when it hit the ground. This was clearly another type of animal workers' strike. It was clear that this farmer was absolutely crackers. The man was barmy and this had obviously rubbed off on his animals. As politely as they could, the cow vets said their goodbyes and returned to the train station, knowing that the only thing they had discovered was that the one and only person who appeared to know anything about Upside Down Cow Disease was barmy, crackers, off his rocker, doo lally and quite simply crazy. Fancy animals going on strike! Who had ever heard of such an idea? No, it was clear that the animals had caught some very weird disease.

As the train pulled in to the railway station at the Land Of The Windmills, the two cow vets saw that the problem was just as bad as when they had went away. In the fields all around, the cows were happily lying on their backs with their feet up in the air. The cow vets slowly walked back to the Village At The End Of The World. When they arrived, a meeting was convened of the Violinists' Dairy Co-Operative to see what could be done. The two cow vets related everything that had happened, including the meeting with the farmer at the crossroads at the very centre of the world.

To begin with, all of the other members of the Violinists' Dairy Co-Operative had a bit of a giggle about the cows going on strike but the more they thought about it, the more it became obvious that it was the only idea they had which might work. To be sure, whether it worked or not, it was also their only idea. Could it really be that their cows had gone on strike? Was it something so simple?

How would the violinists be able to explain to the cows that they were going to meet their demands? Hesitantly, one of the vets put up his hand.

"What if we got someone to dress up as a cow to go and tell them?" he said. Everyone agreed that this was an excellent idea. In fact, the two vets would be the perfect people to do it. The one who had suggested the idea could be the front part of the cow and the other vet could be the back part.

The V.A.T.E.O.T.W.A.D.S. (Village At The End Of The World Amateur Dramatic Society) were called to see if they had a spare cow costume and, as luck would have it, they had one which wasn't currently being used. It didn't take long for the two cow vets to get into the costume and to set off for the fields to explain just what was going on.

Each new cow they spoke to met with the same blank look. The cows didn't understand a single word they were saying – this idea wasn't working at all. What made it worse was when one old heifer mistook the two cow vets in the costume for a bull and started fluttering her eyelashes and blowing them kisses.

They needed to go back to the drawing board so the two cow vets returned to the Village At The End Of The World from the fields, closely chased by the cow who had fallen in love with them.

When they arrived, one of the other violinists had a better idea. Instead of trying to tell the cows what they were going to do, they should just do it. They should start straight away. The first thing they would do would be to go around and give every cow a couple of sugar lumps. Even while they were lying on their backs. Then, they would give them a day off milking. In fact since tomorrow was Tuesday, from now on every Tuesday would be a day off milking for the cows. When the violinists went back out to the fields on Wednesday, they would make sure that their hands were warm before they milked the cows.

The Violinists' Dairy Co-Operative bought up the entire village stock of sugar lumps and immediately set off into the fields to give the cows some sugar lumps. The cows, being cows, just looked at them with those watery eyes and said nothing except for an occasional 'moo.'

The next day, the entire Violinists' Dairy Co-Operative took the day off which they enjoyed almost as much as the cows did – some of them read a book, some of them had a barbecue and some of them just lazed around the house all day doing nothing. As they looked up into the fields, they saw that a couple of the cows were standing the right way up.

On the Wednesday, the violinists all made sure that their hands were nice and warm when they returned to the fields with their vases and flower pots and watering cans to milk the cows. They noticed that there were a few more cows standing the right way up. They milked the upside down cows with their nice warm hands and then brought all of the right-way-up cows to the village to be milked by the secret milking machine. The best part was that the milk that came from the right-way-up cows was right-way-up milk. The violinists were so happy they almost cried.

On the Thursday, a few more cows were standing the right way up in the fields so they didn't have to milk so many cows by hand. By the Saturday, all of the cows in all of the fields were all the right way up and they were all producing right way up milk all of the time.

The cow strike was officially over and the Violinists' Dairy Co-Operative was back in business.

election season

In the career of every elected official, there comes a time when their authority must be put to the test. After all, people must decide who they want their leaders to be. It was with merriment and rejoicing that the Village At The End Of The World decided to have an election.

Each resident of the village would get a vote: Chihuahua's mother, father and grandmother, Cyril the cartographer, Mr. Hubert Q. Lion, Wilson, Bob and Joy, each member of the two orchestras that had followed Bob and Joy to the village, Pete the retired caretaker of the

Land Of The Windmills and the five monkeys (Grandpa, Fred, Big Rab, Lonely Jake and The Leaf). The ants (who technically lived outside the village and did not qualify as residents) would have one vote between them since they had their own power structure. This vote would be cast by the King Of The Ants as their representative. Chihuahua would not be allowed to vote since she was still too young.

It was decided, however, that Chihuahua would be the 'Electoral Commissioner.' It would be her job to make sure that the election was fair and that all of the rules were followed. Since nobody had ever sat down and decided on the rules, Chihuahua more or less made them up as she went along.

First, we must go backwards a little to find out why, in fact, the Village At The End Of The World really needed an election. After all, Mr. Hubert Q. Lion and Wilson were doing a perfectly acceptable job of taking care of local affairs. Unfortunately, a trumpet player from one of the orchestras was getting a little too big for his boots and had decided that he could do a much better job as mayor than Mr. Hubert Q. Lion. What he really meant was that

ᴍᴀʀᴋ ᴍᴄᴋɴɪɢʜᴛ

trumpet players have to work hard – all that boring practicing. It would be much more fun to be the mayor who did a little work in the morning and mostly slept in the afternoons.

This trumpet player decided to challenge the mayor to an election. The people would be allowed to choose who they wanted to be their mayor: Mr. Hubert Q. Lion or this young upstart of a trumpet player who was called Ğïùçæþþõ. If only that was a spelling mistake, but it was his real name: Ğïùçæþþõ. It was pronounced 'Guy-Chap-Oh' but it took him forever to write it down with all those funny little letters.

Ğïùçæþþõ was not a particularly nice fellow. He wasn't liked much by all the other musicians in the orchestra. In fact, he was one of those people who doesn't really have many friends. Unfortunately, it was only the people in his own orchestra who knew what he was like. Remember that there was a whole other orchestra and all of the other people in the village to vote as well.

Mr. Hubert Q. Lion, on the other hand, was liked by almost everyone in the village. He was always willing to listen and always willing to help and everyone knew the story of how he had rescued Chihuahua from the ocean. Little did they know that Mr. Hubert Q. Lion had actually been trying to eat Chihuahua on that particular day.

The first thing that must happen in an election is for people to be nominated for the jobs. There were three jobs that people must be elected to in the Village At The End Of The World: mayor, deputy mayor and police commissioner. We already know of the contest for mayor. Luckily, there were no more cheeky trumpet players trying to cause trouble so Wilson and Grandpa were both safe in their jobs. Ğïùçæþþõ was a little sneaky for the nominations. Instead of getting someone else to nominate him, he nominated himself which, as the Electoral Commissioner (Chihuahua) will tell you is a big no-no. However, nobody found out about this, least of all Chihuahua and so the election was necessary. An election date was set for one month. That would give the candidates plenty of time to canvas – to go around talking to people and trying to get their vote.

To begin with, not many people really listened to Ğïùçæþþõ. They didn't really know who he was and they weren't really interested in what he had to say. However, as time went on, people began to realise that he might be saying something worth listening to. He actually had one or two ideas that might help the village.

Things like extending the train line all the way to the village instead of having it stop at the Land Of The Windmills. Things like free milk for everyone from the Co-Operative since they didn't have to pay any taxes on their earnings. Of course the Violinists' Dairy Co-Operative got upset at this to begin with but then they realised how lucky they were – if they were in the Big City, they would have to pay all kinds of taxes. Yes, Ğïùçæþþõ was set to reform the Village At The End Of The World. What they people didn't realise was that everything Ğïùçæþþõ said was just talk – all he wanted was the nice easy job of mayor so that he could sleep in the afternoons.

Mr. Hubert Q. Lion, on the other hand could offer no reform ideas. He was already in the job. He couldn't say "If I get elected, I will do this or that." He was already the mayor and he hadn't really done much. Or had he?

Mr. Hubert Q. Lion sat down to make a list of all of the things that he had done since he became mayor. He knew that this would be the key to beating Ğïùçæþþõ in the election. While Ğïùçæþþõ was frantically running round the village trying to get people to vote for him, he would wait for the perfect moment to spring his surprise on Ğïùçæþþõ. The silly trumpet player based his entire election campaign on how little the lion had done for the village.

For some reason, people like to kiss babies during elections but there was a big problem in the Village At The End Of The World in that there were no babies. In fact, the youngest person in the whole village (not including the ants) was Chihuahua who was quickly growing up. Just once, Ğïùçæþþõ tried to kiss Chihuahua because that is what politicians do during elections but Chihuahua gave him a punch right on the nose. Ğïùçæþþõ had not one but two black eyes for over a week in the middle of his campaign which certainly did nothing to help his chances.

Ğïùçæþþõ went around every house in the village trying to convince people to vote for him. He managed to convince some people while others remained loyal to Mr. Hubert Q. Lion. In every house Ğïùçæþþõ visited, he was given a cup of tea. He had never drank so much tea in his life. All of this hard work was really exhausting him and he couldn't wait for the day when he was the mayor and could spend his time comfortably dozing in his office. Mr. Hubert Q. Lion, on the other hand, was doing just that. He would take care of any business that needed dealt with first thing in the morning and then he would put his feet up on his desk and

take a nap. In this way, the mayor and the deputy mayor whiled away the dreary afternoons.

As the day of the election drew nearer, tensions began to rise. Every day, supporters would come to the mayoral offices to demand why Mr. Hubert Q. Lion wasn't out getting people to vote for him like Ğïùçæþþõ. Mr. Hubert Q. Lion always gave a flimsy excuse and ushered his supporters out of the office so that he could get back to the important business of catching forty winks.

If anything, Ğïùçæþþõ's campaign was gathering speed. All over the village there were posters, stickers and badges with Ğïùçæþþõ's face on them pronouncing that change was about to come. Every time Ğïùçæþþõ saw one of his posters, he said to himself, "It certainly is – it's going to be me sleeping in that mayor's chair instead of that lazy, no-good, layabout of a lion." Never once did he say this out loud though – he knew that people would never vote for him if they knew what he was really thinking.

The election loomed still closer and closer. Chihuahua was rushed off her feet making sure that she knew how the election was going to take place and that both candidates (Ğïùçæþþõ and Mr. Hubert Q. Lion) were conducting a fair campaign. Actually, she only had to make sure that Ğïùçæþþõ was conducting a fair campaign since

Mr. Hubert Q. Lion didn't seem to be doing anything except snoozing.

On the day before the election, when Ğïùçæþþõ was wrapping up his campaign, Mr. Hubert Q. Lion suddenly woke up and appeared in the village square. He was roaring and shouting and soon a crowd had gathered. He said that all good elections must have a debate between the candidates. He had decided that there would be a debate on the village green that night at 7:00pm and that he, Mr. Hubert Q. Lion, would demonstrate why he was a much better candidate than Ğïùçæþþõ.

It didn't take long for word to reach Ğïùçæþþõ about what had happened. After all, the Village At The End Of The World was a very small village. Ğïùçæþþõ had seen Mr. Hubert Q. Lion's campaign so far and he agreed to take part in the debate.

By seven o'clock that evening, the village green had been transformed. As the Electoral Commissioner, Chihuahua had organised everything. There was a big desk where she would sit as the chairman (or chair-child). There were seats on each side for Mr. Hubert Q. Lion and for Ğïùçæþþõ. There was some

where for them to stand when they were talking.
Seats had been collected from everyone's houses
for the people to sit on and listen.

At seven o'clock precisely, Chihuahua sat
down behind her big desk. She was closely
followed by Mr. Hubert Q. Lion and Ğïùçæþþõ.
As the current mayor, Mr. Hubert Q. Lion was
asked to speak first but he said that he preferred to
wait to see what Ğïùçæþþõ would tell the people.

Ğïùçæþþõ jumped to his feet and began his
speech. There was no doubt about it – Ğïùçæþþõ
was a talented speaker. He shouted and
whispered, made jokes, cajoled, teased and
wittered on and on about how Mr. Hubert Q. Lion
had done nothing for the village. Where were the
roads? The railways? The electricity supply?
The running water? Mr. Hubert Q. Lion had done
nothing for the Village At The End Of The World
apart from nap all morning, snooze all afternoon
and sleep all night. When he was finished, the
audience sat in stunned silence. It was true – Mr.
Hubert Q. Lion hadn't really done much in all his
time as mayor of the Village At The End Of The
World.

Slowly, Mr. Hubert Q. Lion, the mayor,
rose to his feet and approached the podium. In his
paw, he had a single sheet of paper which he
simply set on the podium and walked away, off
the stage and back to his office.

Chihuahua wasn't quite sure what to do – this was most irregular. After all, Mr. Hubert Q. Lion had been the one to call the debate but everyone in the audience was clearly desperate to know what was written on the piece of paper that was now left on the podium. They waited in anticipation before it slowly dawned on Chihuahua that really she was the one who ought to read it out. She climbed the podium, cleared her throat and began to speak...

"It's a list. I'll just read them out one by one. There's no other writing on it except for the list..."

1. I rescued Chihuahua when she was about to fall over the edge of the world
2. I saved the deputy mayor from freezing in the middle of the night, even though I knew he had come to shoot me
3. I averted a plague of ants of biblical proportions that almost wiped out our village. The ants are still our friends
4. I improved culture in our village by the introduction of not one but two symphony orchestras, including the inauguration of the Greatest Concert In The World
5. I successfully campaigned for a police force in our village which has kept not one but two percussion sections under control
6. I organised the rescue again of Chihuahua who had accidentally gone into the Giant's Desert
7. I made three promises when I became mayor: to never eat a human being, to always fight to save a resident of the Village At The End of the World and to always stay here. I have never broken any one of these three promises.

Signed,

Mr. Hubert P. Lion

Some of the ladies in the audience were
having a little bit of a cry to themselves. Some of
the men in the audience were having a little bit of
a cry too but they were (as usual) pretending that
they had something in their eye. The list was right
– Mr. Hubert Q. Lion had done plenty for the
village.

The next day was the day that they had all
been waiting for: election day. There was no
more time for kissing babies of for having
debates. There was no more time to convince
people to vote for you. Today was the day when
people had to cast their votes.

Chihuahua had decided that there was no
point wasting time with silly bits of paper and
ballot boxes and counts and recounts. As
Electoral Commissioner, she had told
everyone to gather on the
village green at noon. All of the
chairs were gone. The podium
was gone and even the big table
that Chihuahua had sat at last night
was gone. Instead, there was a big red
line painted right down the middle of
the green. Chihuahua explained
that if you wanted to vote for Mr.
Hubert Q. Lion, you should stay
on this side of the line. If you
wanted to vote for Ğïùçæþþõ, then
you should go on the other side of

the line.   To illustrate her point, she made
Ğïùçæþþõ go over to the other side of the line and
made Mr. Hubert Q. Lion stay just where he was.
Everyone seemed to understand perfectly so the
election began.

There was much discussion and arguing,
chattering and at one point fighting although the
Village At The End Of The World Police
Department soon sorted that out.   Eventually,
everyone was on the side of the line where they
wanted to be. As they looked around, they could
see that the only people on the other side were
Ğïùçæþþõ and the two men who play the big
drums with the hairy arms and the big, red faces.
The men who play the big drums were in deep
discussion with one another and it was obvious
that the election could not be declared until this
problem had been sorted out.

Chihuahua soon joined their discussion to
find out what was going on and quite soon, they
sheepishly crossed over the line to vote for Mr.
Hubert Q. Lion.   It turned out that they had
forgotten their hearing aids. When Chihuahua had
said, "If you want to vote for Ğïùçæþþõ, then you
should go on the other side of the line," they
thought she had said, "If you want a plate of
spaghetti, then you should go on the other side of
the line."

Mr. Hubert Q. Lion had won the election
fair and square because he truly was the best

person for the job. He didn't go back to sleeping all day right away though – Ğïùçæþþõ had given him some good ideas and he wanted to see if they would work for the village.

Ğïùçæþþõ on the other hand was furious. He had to go back to playing his trumpet and doing all of that boring practicing. He had no time to nap in the afternoon and to make matters worse, the men who play the big drums with the hairy arms and the big, red faces kept teasing him and saying, "Can I have a plate of spaghetti please?"

lions and sealions

Every epic tale (such as this one) must have a final, spectacular battle. It's a rule. No, really – you can check it for yourself. On page 2,745 in *The Laws of Writing Epic Tales*, paragraph three says, 'Every epic tale must have a final, spectacular battle.'

OK, so I made that bit up and it's not at the end of the book either but we don't want to quibble over that and we certainly don't want to hear pretty stories about princesses and butterflies, do we? We want battles and fighting and baddies and heroes, right? What I say is, 'Enough of this sappy, lovery-dovery stuff. Let's get to the fighting!' Maybe that's because I'm a boy. Girls:

don't worry, keep reading because there's a sappy lovery-dovery story coming next.

One morning, Bob and Joy got up early to help the Violinists' Dairy Co-Operative with the milking. If you've ever lived on a farm, you'll know that the milking is done very early in the morning. So early, in fact, that it is often still dark by the time it is finished. When they were done, Bob and Joy decided they would go to the beach to watch the sunrise. After all, they were really in love and that is the kind of thing that people who are in love do (Yuck! I bet they even sometimes give each other a kiss on the lips!).

As Bob and Joy sat on a sand dune looking out to the ocean at the end of the world, they saw a very strange sight. You see, they had never, ever seen any creature in the sea. No fish or octopus, no jellyfish or crabs, no shrimps and not even any seaweed. Today, however, sitting on a rock sunning himself was a huge sealion. He had big whiskers and two long tusks. He was clearly enjoying the Autumn sunshine and didn't really take much notice of Bob and Joy as they watched him. If only, Bob and Joy had ran to the mayor's office straight away, they might have saved the Village At The End Of The World from what was about to happen. Yet there is no point in singing our could-of-should-of-

mark mcknight

would-of's when it is too late to do anything about it.

The next morning, after the milking was finished, Bob and Joy once again watched the sun rise up over the ocean and as it got lighter and lighter, they realised that there were now two huge sealions sunning themselves on the rocks. To have seen one sealion was something interesting. To see two at once was really rather special. Bob and Joy had never before seen such a thing. Since they lived in the Village At The End Of The World, though, they were a little too used to strange things happening (they did, after all, once have a symphony orchestra each to provide soundtracks for their lives) and they did not report the two sealions to the proper authorities.

This format of events continued for quite some time – Bob and Joy would go to the beach to watch the sun rise after they had finished helping with the milking and each day there would be another sealion sunning himself on the rocks with big whiskers and two long tusks.

Of course, as the number of sealions grew, so did the noise and it wasn't long before most of the village had heard the sealions for themselves and come to the beach to investigate – attracted by the incredible din that these sealions were making. Of course, Bob and Joy had known for

143

weeks but they just hadn't thought it worth their while to tell anyone.

Eventually, word reached the mayor, Mr. Hubert Q. Lion who straight away padded to the beach to find out exactly what was happening. As he arrived on the beach, he was overwhelmed by the number of sealions who had now congregated on the beach – there were loads of them. The mayor could already sense that this might end in disaster – sealions had a reputation the world over as very stubborn and rude creatures. Mr. Hubert Q. Lion would have to handle this very carefully otherwise it might turn into a war between lions and sealions.

The problem with sealions is that they don't have a king. They don't even have a prince or a sultan or a prime minister or a chairman or a chief or a shah or a pharaoh or any sort of boss whatsoever. Sealions each do exactly what they please and it was clear that all of these sealions felt like sunning themselves on the beach beside the Village At The End Of The World.

Why, you might ask was this a problem? Have you ever lived near a sealion beach? For a start, sealions stink. You would too if all you did was eat fish and sleep all day. One sealion stinks. Hundreds of sealions together positively reek. Already, the whole village stank of sealion – that curious mix of fish and wet fur. For another thing,

mark mcknight

they are forever wandering all
over the place. Already, a few had
ventured into the village square
and sealions were rude to just about everyone they
met, including other sealions. In fact, sealions
were well known for two things: being rude and
fighting. As you can see, having a beach full of
sealions was not acceptable to the Village At The
End Of The World Village Council. Mr. Hubert
Q. Lion, as their elected representative, was
therefore compelled to deal with it.

Climbing the tallest dune on the beach, Mr.
Hubert Q. Lion tried to address the sealions to see
why they had decided to stop on this particular
beach. One or two sealions snorted and rolled
over. Another couple flicked some sand in the air
with their flippers and then rolled over. Most just
ignored him. One or two slowly flopped their
way down the beach and back in to the water. It
was clear that Mr. Hubert Q. Lion was not getting
anywhere. In fact, none of the sealions were even
listening to him.

Mr. Hubert Q. Lion returned to his office
dejectedly. What was he to do? He had tried to
talk to the sealions, to reason with them, and they
had ignored him completely. Clearly this was
going to need a creative solution.

The mayor's first port of call was the
Village At The End Of The World Police Station.
Maybe Grandpa, as the police commissioner

would have an idea. Mr. Hubert Q. Lion and Grandpa walked together to survey the beach. These two old friends looked sombrely over what had once been a very beautiful place that was now blotted by lots of rude sealions. Things were not all lost, however, for Grandpa had a couple of ideas that were worth a try.

Grandpa quickly ran back to the police station, for there was no time to lose. He gathered his troop of monkeys: Fred, Big Rab, Lonely Jake and The Leaf and explained his plan. The monkeys gathered as many pairs of handcuffs as they could find and set off for the beach. The plan was to arrest as many sealions as possible and put them in the Village At The End Of The World County Jail. There would be no trial – this was internment. Unfortunately, when they arrived at the beach, they discovered that their handcufffs would not fit onto the flippers of a sealion. The sealions just laughed at these monkeys who were trying to arrest them without any handcuffs. After a few minutes, the monkeys realised that they would have to give up – the sealions were beginning to get restless and the monkeys knew they wouldn't have a chance if a fight broke out.

Grandpa was not yet out of ideas, however. His idea with the monkeys had failed miserably but his next idea he thought would work for sure. Since the sealions made so much noise, he would beat

them at their own game. He called the men who play the big drums with the hairy arms and the big, red faces into his office and explained the plan. The men both left their hearing aids with Grandpa, collected their drums and set off for the beach.

The sealions heard the men coming from a long way off and they knew that they would have a fight on their hands. Each sealion took a deep breath and began making as much noise as they could: they bellowed and whooped and flapped their tails on the sand and in the sea. Soon, the whole beach was almost vibrating with the racket that the sealions were making. When the men who play the big drums with the hairy arms and the big, red faces finally arrived at the beach, the sealions were twice as loud as they were which was really something quite incredible. Even without their hearing aids, the men who play the big drums had never heard something so loud and they too had to return to the village having failed to get rid of the sealions.

Grandpa had one more idea. If this didn't work, then he was out of ideas. This time, he called the King of the Ants and explained his idea. In spite of his apprehension, the King of the Ants gathered every single ant in the colony and prepared to go to war – all eight billion, five hundred and eighty nine million, nine hundred and

thirty four thousand, five hundred and ninety two of them. "This," said the king, "is the kind of thing that ants do!"
The ants marched to the beach in attack formation. They were ready for the sealions. They would be the ones to defeat the sealions. Then, disaster struck! Just before they reached the beach, they came to a small trickle of a stream that wasn't very wide at all.

Mr. Hubert Q. Lion, Grandpa and the monkeys and the men who play the big drums with the hairy arms could step over this little stream in one step. The problem was that although the little stream was only this size...

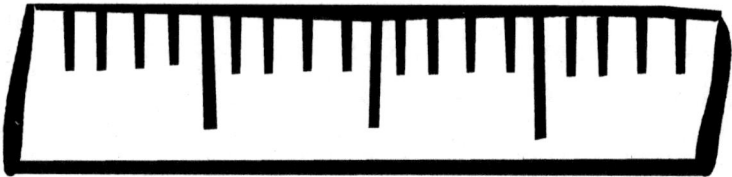

...an ant is only this size...

...and so, the King of the Ants and all eight billion, five hundred and eighty nine million, nine hundred and thirty four thousand, five hundred and ninety two were forced to turn back because they couldn't even get to the beach.

As Mr. Hubert Q. Lion and Grandpa watched the ants slowly march back through the village, they knew that they were now in big trouble. None of their ideas had worked. They had tried everything they could think of and the rude sealions were still sunning themselves on the beach.

There was nothing else for it: they made a cup of tea, since tea always helps you to think. It was as Mr. Hubert Q. Lion finished his third cup that he had his idea. He realised that for it to work, he would have to eat a big slice of humble pie but it was just about crazy enough to work.

There is one thing in this world that sealions hate more than anything else and Mr. Hubert Q. Lion knew just where he could find some. The mayor needed a meeting behind closed doors with the five original residents of the Village At The End Of The World: Chihuahua, her mother, father and grandmother and Cyril the cartographer. Grandpa and the rest of the police force were assigned to make sure nobody was listening.

The problem was that Mr. Hubert Q. Lion would have to return to the Big City but he had made a promise many years before that he would never leave the Village At The End Of The World. After much negotiation, Baz and Cyril eventually agreed that this was a time of dire emergency and in this case, it would be OK to break the promise. Chihuahua's mother and grandmother were not convinced. They thought that when Mr. Hubert Q. Lion returned to the Big City, he would stay there. They would not accept any assurances. For the first time ever, since the votes were equal, Chihuahua was allowed a say in the matter. She was growing into quite a big girl now and she had already been the Electoral Commissioner so it was time her opinion mattered. After a long pause for thought, Chihuahua said she thought the mayor should go. After all, no other idea had worked.

That very day, Mr. Hubert Q. Lion set off to catch the milk train that was bound for the Big City. Soon enough, he had arrived and made his way to that same field where our story first began: the field full of butterflies where he found the same princess playing with the butterflies as she had always done. Of course, she was much older now just like Mr. Hubert Q. Lion. In case you have forgotten, the princess tricked the lion into having a race to the end of the world and back.

When the lion saw the princess was there already, he assumed that she had won the race. After all, he had spent all of that time working as the mayor of the Village At The End Of The World. When the princess saw the lion, she thought she was in big trouble – after all, she hadn't even

been to the end of the world. She had only gone to the end of the street and waited until the lion was out of sight before she came back to play with her butterflies.

Wilson (the retired hunter and deputy mayor) had told Mr. Hubert Q. Lion many times the story of how he had arrived in the village – how he had actually been to all four villages at the end of the world: one with a rhinoceros for mayor, another with an ostrich, another with a frog and of course their own village with a lion for mayor. As Mr. Hubert Q. Lion talked with the princess, it was clear that she had not been to the end of the world. When she told him that she had met the mayor at the end of the world and that he was a lovely man, he knew she was lying and he told her so. It was only then that he realised he had been tricked.

Mr. Hubert Q. Lion remembered the sealions. This was not the time to worry about being tricked. His village was in trouble and he needed the princess' help. The princess knew that he knew she had tricked him and, for fear of having her head bitten off, was only too willing to help. Mr. Hubert Q. Lion, the princess and all the butterflies returned to the railway station to travel back to the Village At The End Of The World.

Soon enough, the lion, the princess and the butterflies were walking back through the Village

At The End Of The World. They soon had a crowd following them because everyone knew what was going to happen. You see, it is well known that sealions simply cannot stand butterflies. It's funny, because almost everyone else in the whole world really loves butterflies – they are so pretty and colourful. For some reason though, sealions refuse to be around butterflies. Maybe it's because sealions are such a boring brown colour while the butterflies get all the different prettier colours.

As Mr. Hubert Q. Lion and the princess came over the sand dune, the sealions either ignored them completely or once again snorted and rolled over. They weren't expecting what happened next. Not just hundreds, or even thousands, but millions of butterflies flew over the dune. There were so many beautiful colours: red, yellow, green, orange, pink, blue and everything in between.

Most of the sealions were lolling around with their eyes half shut but when they saw the butterflies, without a word every single one of them flopped their way as quickly as they could back to the ocean. As the last one jumped in the water, he shouted, "You've won this time but we'll be back!"

However, Mr. Hubert Q. Lion invited the princess and her butterflies to stay. After all, the princess was very pretty and the butterflies decided that they really loved to be beside the ocean. From that day forward, the princess lived in a little house beside the beach so that she could play with her butterflies all day long and the sea lions were much too scared to come back to the beach because of the princess and all her butterflies.

wedding bells at last

If it's a love story you want, then it's a love story you shall get. Bob and Joy met each other when they both won a very odd competition to have a symphony orchestra to provide music to accompany their lives. Some may call it destiny and others may call it fate. For a little while now, they have been thinking about getting married. There were two problems as far as they could see. Firstly, there was no preacher in the Village At The End Of The World to perform the marriage ceremony. This was, however, not the biggest problem. The biggest problem was that there was no church in the Village At The End Of The

World. No church meant no church bells and what kind of a wedding would it be without wedding bells?

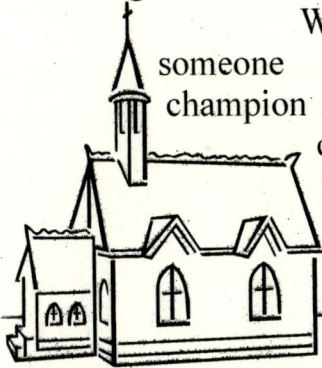

What they needed was for someone in local government to champion their cause, to fight their corner. Joy had approached her father (the deputy mayor) once or twice but he had been more interested in napping than in building a church. One day, however, something happened to change all of that. In fact, it has already happened. You've already witnessed it.

You see, what I didn't mention before was that the princess was in actual fact a lion princess. When Mr. Hubert Q. Lion invited Princess Lydia to stay in the Village At The End Of The World with her butterflies, it wasn't only to protect the beach from the sealions. He had already fallen in love with her and she had already fallen in love with him. While they were on the train on the way from the Big City to save the village from the sealions, they had been talking and realised that they had a lot in common. They were, after all, both lions and that was just for starters.

Soon, as Wilson the deputy mayor had his afternoon nap, Mr. Hubert Q. Lion would go to the beach to spend his afternoons with Princess

Lydia. This was a very big thing because everyone knew just how much Mr. Hubert Q. Lion really loved to snooze in the afternoons.

It wasn't long after that Mr. Hubert Q. Lion was spending every afternoon at the beach. It wasn't long after that again Mr. Hubert Q. Lion was spending his mornings at the beach too. Soon, if people had important things they needed to discuss with the mayor, the knew to go to the beach instead of the mayoral offices because they knew he wouldn't be there anyway.

Eventually, Grandpa was the one who suggested that Mr. Hubert Q. Lion should propose to the princess. One Summer evening, just as the sun was sinking down below the horizon, Mr. Hubert Q. Lion got down on one knee with a ring made of the finest gold (that he had sent a flautist to the Big City to buy specially) and said, "Princess Lydia, will you make me the happiest lion in the world by becoming my wife?"

Princess Lydia thought for just a moment which seemed like an age to Mr. Hubert Q. Lion and said one simple word, "Yes!" They were so happy that they played with the butterflies all day long. Word soon spread around the village that Mr. Hubert Q. Lion and Princess Lydia were to be married. When Bob and Joy heard the good news, they knew that maybe this could be what they

needed so that they could have their wedding too. If the mayor was getting married then they would build a church with bells and everything in double quick time.

Straight away, Bob and Joy went to the beach to explain their problem once again to the two lions: there was no preacher to conduct the ceremony and there was no church which meant no church bells and what is the use of a wedding without wedding bells?

Mr. Hubert Q. Lion thought for a moment and then, for the first time in over a month, he returned to his office and set to work. He wanted his wedding to be perfect for Princess Lydia and if that meant building a church in the Village At The End Of The World, then so be it.

Within an hour, work had begun on building the church. First, the men who play the big drums with the hairy arms and the big, red faces dug the foundations. Next, the ants began construction. They were so used to building their ant hills that the walls were up in no time. After that, the Village At The End Of The World Police Department began work on the roof of the church. They were so used to climbing trees that they didn't even need any ladders. By the end of one week, the church was almost complete. It was perfect: whitewashed walls, little wooden pews for the people to sit on, a pulpit for the preacher to preach from and best of all, lots of flowers that the butterflies brought, ready for two weddings.

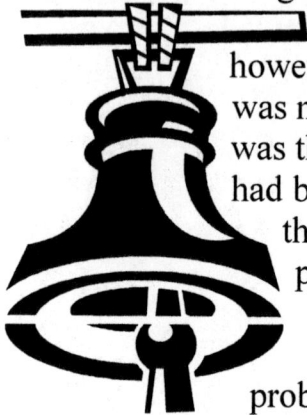

The church was, however, only almost complete. It was missing one critical thing and that was the church bells. The ant builders had built a big tower on the church so that there would be somewhere to put the bell. The monkeys had hung the ropes that would be used to ring the bells. The problem was that nobody in the whole village knew anything whatsoever about bells. Of course, they all knew what a bell looked like and sounded like. They just didn't have a clue how to even start to make one or even if you could buy them in a shop.

This was a very big problem indeed. With the church complete, Mr. Hubert Q. Lion and Princess Lydia fixed the date for their wedding. Bob and Joy fixed the date for their wedding too. Oddly enough, they picked the same date and the same time. Instead of arguing about it, they decided to have a joint wedding ceremony. All they could do was hope and pray that somehow they would have the bells ready by then.

As is often the case in a wedding, the ladies (Joy and Princess Lydia) set about organising the

details. What would they eat at the reception? Who would be invited? Most importantly, they set off on a shopping trip to the Big City to be measured and fitted for their wedding dresses. They also used the trip to buy some new shoes and one or two other bits and pieces: a handbag, some smelly things and a big bag of sweets.

Mr. Hubert Q. Lion and Bob were left in the Village At The End Of The World to find a solution to the problem of the church bells. They now had a church but no church bells and what is the use of a wedding without wedding bells? They tried thinking in the mayor's office. They tried thinking at the beach. They went to the Land Of The Windmills to see if they could think there. Still, they could think of no solution to their problem. The church had no church bells and nobody knew anything about how to make one or get one. The best suggestion that anybody had come up with was to steal one from somewhere. Apart from being against the law, no-one even knew where they could steal one from!

Quite by chance, while Princess Lydia and Joy were in the Big City on their shopping expedition, they met a very strange man. For a start, he was completely deaf. He couldn't hear a single thing. The only way he could communicate was by writing things down in a little notebook. The only was you could talk to him was by writing it down in the same notebook. What made him so interesting was that the reason he was so deaf was that he had spent all his life making bells. When he tested them, they were so big and so loud that he had eventually become deaf.

Joy and Princess Lydia almost fell over themselves when they found this out. A  bellmaker was just what they were looking for in the Village At The End Of The World. Yet nothing they could do or say would convince the bellmaker to return to the Village At The End Of The World with them. Even the offer of a free train ride didn't appeal to him. It was then that Joy had an idea. She wrote something very neatly in the man's notebook and without any hesitation, he wrote four words, 'When do we go?'

As Joy, Princess Lydia and the bellmaker arrived back in the Village At The End Of The World, the women of the village looked from their doorways and said what they always say at times like this, "Hrumph! Typical! Womenfolk always having to solve the mens' problems!"

The bellmaker began his work right away – there was no time to lose. He gathered up all the percussion players from both orchestras as his apprentices – they were used to beating things and that's exactly how you go about making a bell. You have to beat all the metal into the right shape. Little did they know that this bellmaking was the humble beginning of the Village At The End Of The World's second most important industry. Second only to the Violinists' Dairy Co-Operative of course.

The bellmaker's makeshift workshop was set up on one side of the village green. There would be hammering in the morning, hammering in the evening and hammering at night. After all, they had to make seventeen bells of different sizes, all in time for the wedding.

Baz set up his workshop once again on the other side of the green and once again began work on his invention. Little did he know that this would be the continuation of the Village At The End Of The World's third most important industry: hearing aid manufacture. This time, however, since the bellmaker was completely deaf, the hearing aid would have to be super powered and so work began in earnest on the new and improved hearing aid.

The village green was a jumble of old bits of metal, electrical cables, bits of broken radios, an old typewriter, a few bits of railway track that had been left over when they Big City Railroad Corporation build the railway and all kinds of other junk. It was almost as if Baz and the bellmaker were having two separate competitions: the first to see who could make the most noise and the second to see who could make the biggest mess.

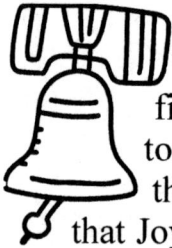

As the days whizzed by, time was getting shorter and shorter to firstly finish all of the bells and get them to the church on time and secondly finish the bellmaker's hearing aid. The deal that Joy had made with the bellmaker was that if he could build and install the seventeen bells in time for the wedding, then he would have his hearing aid on the same day.

It seemed like every day, another bell came out of the bellmaker's workshop and was very slowly and carefully carried to the church. The monkeys were in charge of getting the bell in to the tower and ready to ring. When each bell was installed, it was rung just once to make sure it was working. Mr. Hubert Q. Lion had said that he wanted the first time the bells were rung properly to be the day of the wedding.

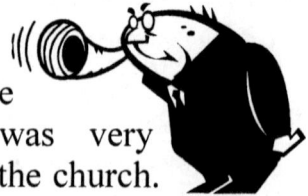

By the day before the wedding, sixteen bells were in the church ready to ring. There was, however, a serious problem. The biggest bell was the one that was missing. They had run out of metal to finish the final bell. This was a crisis.

On the same day, Baz was almost finished his hearing aid but he too had run out of old bits and pieces that he needed to finish. Neither workshop was going to meet its deadline.

Mr. Hubert Q. Lion and Princess Lydia were busy preparing for their wedding. Bob and Joy were busy preparing for their wedding. Both Baz and the bellmaker decided that they would not trouble the happy couples on the day before the wedding. They both arrived at the door of the mayor's office at the same time to see if the deputy mayor had any ideas about what they could do.

As they sat in the mayor's office discussing the problem, Wilson had an idea: an idea that would be the perfect solution to both these men's problems. Yet an idea that would be an unbearable heartbreak for this hunter, a man of the wild who's best friend for many years had been his shotgun.

Wilson asked for a moment alone and then he would give both the men what they needed. Baz and the bellmaker waited outside the office door while inside, they thought they heard the old man crying.

    After the two men had left the office, the deputy mayor slowly took his shotgun from above the fireplace. This had been his friend and companion for many years. His wife, the only true love of his life and mother to his daughter, Joy, had died many years ago. He had used this gun to bring down all kinds of beast. The only animal he had never killed was a lion. This gun was the one thing that right now could bring the greatest happiness to his daughter. The metal in the barrel of the gun would be just enough to complete the final bell for the church. The firing mechanism would be just what Baz needed to finish his hearing aid to pay the bellmaker. But this gun was also something that he could not bear to destroy. His gun and his daughter were the only two things that he cared about in this world. He simply could not believe what he was about to do.

    Wilson called Baz and the bellmaker back in to the mayor's office and slowly, without a word, handed them the shotgun. Both men could see the tears in the old hunter's eyes and departed without a word – there was nothing to be said.

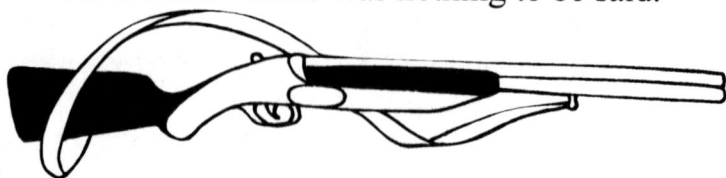

mark mcknight

Before long, the gun had been cut into two pieces: the mechanism for Baz and the barrel for the bellmaker.

The next morning, the church bells pealed for the first time. Everyone in the village knew that today was a very special day. They had their own church with seventeen bells, the mayor was about to be married and so were Bob and Joy. For the first time in a long time, the bellmaker was able to hear the bells he had made thanks to his new super-powered hearing aid.

It was on the morning of the weddings that they realised they had only solved one of the problems that was stopping them from getting married. They had a church with bells in it but what use was a wedding if you didn't have a preacher to conduct the ceremony. Word of this problem spread round the village faster than wildfire.

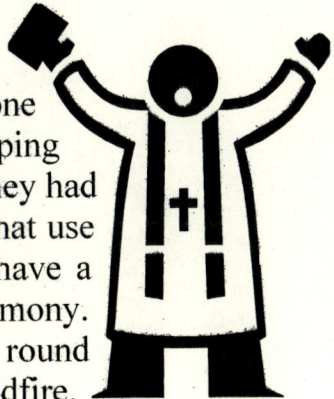

What a to-do! They had solved the big problem and forgotten about the little one. It was too late to get a preacher from the Big City. They were really stuck. Everyone was already in the church waiting for the ceremony to begin. The bell ringers were getting tired – they couldn't go on for much longer.

Only then did Wilson admit that he had been a preacher before Joy had been born. He had never told anyone in the village. When his wife had died, he couldn't go on any longer as a preacher and that is why he had become a hunter. With tears of happiness in his eyes, Joy's father conducted the marriage ceremony first for Mr. Hubert Q. Lion and Princess Lydia and then for his own daughter, Joy and Bob, the love of her life.

The only two people who ever knew how great a sacrifice the deputy mayor had made for his own daughter were Baz and the bellmaker. Joy never found out although she often wondered what had happened to her father's gun that used to hang above the fireplace in his office.

the first annual village at the end of the world beard competition

After all of these strange and upsetting goings on in the Village At The End Of The World, Mr. Hubert Q. Lion decided that they needed to do something that was purely fun in the village. Something that everyone could take part in (or the men at least). After all, they had managed to get rid of the sealions, the cows were cured from their upside down disease (the Violinists' Dairy Co-Operative hadn't dared to tell

anyone that the cows had been on strike) and they had just made it through a very stressful election.

Mr. Hubert Q. Lion announced from the announcing box (an upturned soap box in the middle of the village green) that he was inaugurating the First Annual Village At The End Of The World Beard Competition. There would be prizes for the longest beard, the most artistic beard and for the cleanest beard. Women could enter the competition for fun with false beards if they wanted but they would not be eligible for any prizes. The competition would be open only to humans – lions, monkeys and ants were not eligible but would comprise the judging panel as they were, as far as beards were concerned, entirely unbiased.

On that day, the entire village stopped shaving. The violinists, Bob, the men who play the big drums with the hairy arms and the big, red faces, Cyril the Cartographer, Baz, Wilson, Pete who used to oil the windmills and even the two conductors. In fact, every man in the village stopped shaving.

To be honest, nobody really noticed anything for a day or two. Day number three of the beard competition was when thing really started to be a problem. For a start, the wives didn't like it – they didn't want to give their

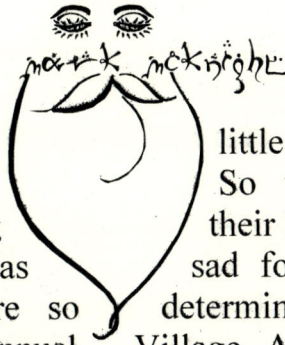

mark mcknight

husbands a little kiss with all of that stubble. So the wives just stopped giving their husbands a little kiss. This was sad for the husbands but they were so determined to win the First Annual Village At The End Of The World Beard Competition that they really didn't mind so much.

The next problem that came was with the children. The children always like to play as if they are grown up and so they began experimenting to give themselves a beard. Even the girls! Since the men only had some stubble to begin with, they would wipe some mud on their chin to make it look like they had stubble too but as the mens' beards grew longer and longer, the children wanted longer and longer beards too. They began to use all kinds of things to give themselves beards. The most popular, or course was sheep's wool. The problem was that the wool was white so they had to change the colour to make it look like a real beard. For brown, they used mud. For black they used blackberries. For ginger they used rotten carrots. Don't even ask me what they used to make blond beards! Can you imaging an entire classroom full of children with fake beards that stink of mud, blackberries and rotten carrots? Can you imagine trying to teach children like that?

Of course, the women of the village were not to be outdone by either the men or the children. Those ladies with long hair would clip it in such a way that it came round onto their chin and looked just like a beard. Those who didn't mostly resorted to the same kinds of tricks as the children, although usually they used much less fragrant things to dye their fake beards.

Yes, the Village At The End Of The World had really taken this beard competition to heart. It wasn't long before even those who weren't technically allowed to enter the competition were wearing fake beards. The entire Village At The End Of The World Police Department were sporting some very well made fake beards that would have looked almost real if they weren't being worn by a monkey. Even the ants were in on the act: they each wore a tiny fake beard. They were so cute with their little whiskers. The only person in the whole village who didn't wear a beard was Mr. Hubert Q. Lion although in fairness, he did have his own mane which I suppose is a kind of beard.

Beards, beards, beards. They were everywhere. The bellmakers had them, the Violinists's Dairy Co-Operative had them, the butterflies had them and if you took the time to

marek mcknight

travel to the Land Of The Windmills, even the windmills had them!

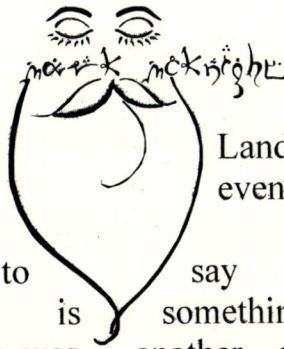

Well, to say beards were everywhere is something of a mistake. You see, there was another person in the village who did not wear a beard. That person was Chihuahua's mother. You see, the woman had beardophobia which means that she was absolutely petrified of people with a beard. If she saw someone wearing a beard (fake or otherwise), she would run away screaming because she was so scared. While the rest of the village was having a whale of a time with the First Annual Village At The End Of The World Beard Competition, Chihuahua's mother was beside herself with worry. She had reached the stage where she couldn't go outside any more because everyone she saw had a beard and she would have to run screaming all the way home.

No matter how much Chihuahua pleaded, her mother would not let her wear a beard like all of her friends. What Chihuahua's mother didn't know was that as soon as she walked out the door, Chihuahua would put on her fake beard to walk to school. She would always remember to take it off again before she came home in the evening though. Otherwise, she would be in big trouble.

Despite numerous complaints to both the police and the mayor of the Village At The End

Of The World, mother could not cancel the beard competition planned since she who had a problem – Chihuahua's convince them to competition. The would go ahead as was the only one everyone else loved the idea.

One afternoon, Chihuahua decided that it was time for her mother to get over her beardophobia. The only way to get over your fears, Chihuahua had heard, was to face them. If you are scared of heights, then you should go somewhere very high. If you are frightened of spiders then you should hold one in your hand. If you are terrified of beards, then you should grow one yourself. At least that is what Chihuahua had decided in her head.

As her mother lay sleeping on the sofa in their living room, Chihuahua very quietly got her own fake beard. Very delicately, she put it on her mother's face and carefully put the elastic behind her head so that it wouldn't fall off.

A couple of hours later, her mother woke up and got ready to prepare dinner. She pottered around the kitchen getting a few things ready – peeling some potatoes, heating some oil in a pan to cook the meat. She obviously didn't realise that she was wearing the fake beard. Soon, she realised that she had no vegetables for the meal so she sent Chihuahua to the shop next door for some carrots.

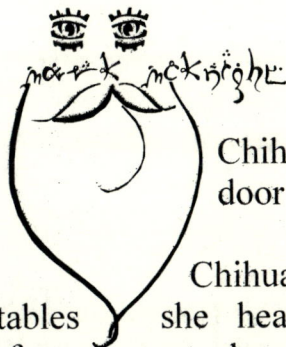

While Chihuahua was paying for the vegetables she heard the loudest shriek coming from next door. Her mother must have finally discovered the beard. Giggling all the way, Chihuahua ran back to her house and found her mother standing looking at herself in the mirror with her mouth opening and closing like a goldfish.

Nothing Chihuahua could do would get her mother back to the kitchen to finish dinner. It was like she was stuck looking at her beard in the mirror. Chihuahua knew she had gone too far with this joke but she was too scared to tell her mother the truth. She would be in serious trouble if she did that. There was nothing else for it: Chihuahua went to the kitchen and cooked the rest of the dinner herself.

By bed time, Chihuahua's mother was still standing in front of the mirror doing her goldfish impression. Chihuahua did, however, manage to get her mother in to bed.

The next morning, Chihuahua's mother was back in the real world again. She was heartbroken that she had grown a beard. How could this have happened? Every time she saw her reflection, she shrieked again but as the day wore on, she was getting more and more used to having a beard. In fact, the more more she like it – and warm if you the cold and it was wanted to stroke didn't have a cat. she had it, the a beard was nice had to go out in also useful if you something and

By nightfall, Chihuahua's mother had more or less got used to the idea of having a beard. It was, after all, something that men had to put up with all of the time anyway. Maybe it wasn't so bad.

As Chihuahua's mother was getting used to her beard, the date of the First Annual Village At The End Of The World Beard Competition was drawing closer and closer. The men of the village had invented all kinds of potions and lotions which, they swore, were going to make their beards grow longer, faster and cleaner than anyone else's.

Unfortunately, some of these potions had some interesting side effects which two tuba players found out to their discomfort but that is another story entirely.

Finally, after a wait of almost two months, it was the day of the First Annual Village At The End Of The World Beard Competition. There were those who had decided to enter the competition for length and so had simply not shaved whatsoever since the competition had been announced. There were those who had decided to enter the cleanest beard competition and so the had used all manner of cleaning products to try to be cleaner than everyone else. Lastly, there were those who had entered the competition for the most artistic beard. Some had plaits or were tied up with ribbons. Some had flowers woven into their beards. Others had all kinds of twists and turns. One even looked like a giant spike and had some cheese and pineapple chunks on it. Although the men were all around with their real beards, the women and children had also made a special effort with their fake beards and they too were pretending to enter the competitions: long beards, clean beards and artistic beards.

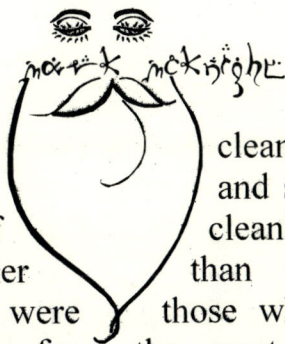

On the village green that day, there was the atmosphere of a festival. There were stalls and music and dancing. There were a hundred different things to eat and drink. There were flowers and bunting and banners everywhere. The whole village had made such an effort for the First Annual Village At The End Of The World Beard Competition that before the competition had even started, Mr. Hubert Q. Lion had decided this would definitely become one of the highlights of his year. It was, after all, to be an annual competition.

As people milled around the green eating, drinking, laughing and having fun, Mr. Hubert Q.

Lion climbed on box in the centre declared that the Village At The Beard Competition to the same soap of the green and First Annual End Of The World was officially open. The judging began in earnest: Mr. Hubert Q. Lion, Grandpa and the King of the Ants were the official judging panel although practically everyone in the green formed their own unofficial judging panels.

Chihuahua's mother, on the other hand was still hiding in her house. She had gotten used to her own beard but she didn't want to see the whole village with their beards. That would just be too much. Yet Chihuahua knew that today would be the day – if her mother didn't get over her fear of beards today, she never would. What Chihuahua had been too scared to tell her mother for over a month now was that the beard she was wearing was not real. Her mother still thought she had grown a real beard.

With much negotiating, cajoling and sweet-talking, Chihuahua finally convinced her mother to go to the village green. After all, the rest of the village was there. Why should she miss out just because her mother she was scared of beards? Chihuahua and her mother set out for the village green. The streets were deserted – everyone was already at the village green having a good time and enjoying the beard competition.

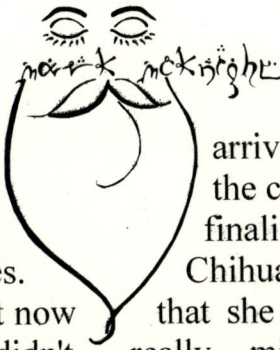

As they arrived, the judges had narrowed the contestants down to three finalists in each of the categories. Chihuahua's mother discovered that now that she had a beard of her own, she didn't really mind the other people who had them, although the women who were wearing fake beards made her feel a little uncomfortable. It just wasn't right.

Finally, the three judges were ready with the winners of all three categories. As Mr. Hubert Q. Lion announced the winners, everyone cheered. The winner of the longest beards was a double bass player, well known as a very hairy man. The winner of the clean competition was Cyril the cartographer, although there had to be an inquiry after some women had tried to enter the competition with fake beards. Last, but not least, the winner of the artistic competition was Wilson, the deputy mayor. His handlebar moustache drooped to a sharpened point on each end and his beard was carefully combed into a beautiful upwards curve. Everyone agreed that his was the most artistic beard possibly in all the world. Even Chihuahua's mother agreed.

The party continued long into the night — there was so much good food to eat and so many great things to drink that there was no reason to go home just yet. Shortly before midnight, Chihuahua thought that it was about time to tell her mother the had worked – her over her fear of Chihuahua sat mother and spoke in would be heard above the music. truth. After all, it mother was now beards.

down beside her her ear so that she

If you had been watching Chihuahua's mother's face, you would have seen it go from a contented smile to a look of fury in two seconds flat. The first thing that the mother did was to rip off her fake beard which she had thought was the real thing for over a month now. Chihuahua knew she was in trouble and so she did what anyone in a similar position would do. She ran. She ran and ran and ran because she was sure her mother would chase her.

But the mother was enjoying herself too much. While Chihuahua spent most of the rest of the evening running through the streets and jumping every time she saw a shadow that she thought was her mother, her mother remained at the party all night enjoying herself.

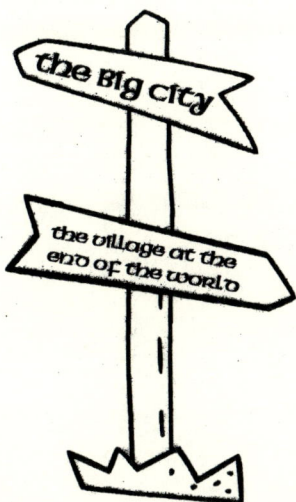

the Big City

the village at the end of the world

happily ever after?

And so we must leave the Village At The End Of The World for if you look very closely, you will find there are no more pages in this book to fill. We must say farewell to the mayor and mayoress, Mr. Hubert Q. and Princess Lydia Lion. We must also say goodbye to the Wilson, the retired hunter and deputy mayor and to Bob and Joy, his daughter and son-in-law. We bid a fond Adieu to the ants, the butterflies, the monkeys and the two symphony orchestras. We must take our leave of Chihuahua and her family – mother, father and grandmother. And Pete and Cyril, we bid thee au revoir.

Pack our bags, travel along the Village At The End Of The World Highway for one week, turn left onto Land Of The Windmills Boulevard and just 2 miles further we see for the last time the unforgettable sight of those many twirling sails.

As we wait on the platform for the milk train that will take us back to the Big City, we wonder, 'Will they really live happily ever after? How will we know?'

With a tear in our eyes, we step on to the train and slowly begin the journey through the Giant's Desert. It is as the train pulls into the Big City Railway Station and we are once again caught up in the bustle of everyday life and we remember that this is not a farewell forever. We can catch the milk train going the opposite direction any day we choose and once again visit the Village At The End Of The World.

As you return to your house in the Big City, you remember that you need to leave a note for the milkman.

No Milk on Tuesday please: it's the cows' day off!

Printed in the United Kingdom
by Lightning Source UK Ltd.
111371UKS00001B/7-75